LOOKING FOR THE TOMB OF ZHANG GT AND HIS WIFE

RESTORE TRUTH

About the Author:

Restore Truth is a distinguished author and former editor-in-chief of a prominent newspaper. A literary figure with deep expertise in both poetry and fiction, Restore Truth is also the Chief Editor of the Modern Chinese Great Dictionary. His contributions to the literary world span multiple genres and languages, establishing him as a notable voice in international literature.

Among Restore Truth's accolades is the first prize for his novel Anecdote Editing, awarded by the "Weekend" competition. His novel The Critic was selected as a textbook in the Chinese-English Translation Tutorial published by Tsinghua University Press, solidifying his role as an educator and cultural bridge.

Restore Truth's extensive literary career reflects a commitment to both his native Chinese heritage and a global literary audience

• Table of Contents •

Chapter 1- From Peking University to Soviet Area 1

Chapter 2- Overthrown by a False Telegram 16

Chapter 3- After Being Overthrown 24

Chapter 4- Madam Yang Zilie 41

Chapter 5- "My Memories" by Zhang Guotao 46

Chapter 6- Toronto 56

Chapter 7- Pine Hills Cemetery 62

Chapter 8- Tombstones of the Couple 67

Chapter 9- Steles of Zhang Guotao 71

Brief Introduction

- - The author takes you on a long journey across mountains and rivers, looking for the tomb of Zhang Guotao and his wife

Zhang Guotao was the early leader of the Communist Party of China. He was also the student leader of the May 4th movement of China, the representative of the First Congress of the Communist Party of China, one of the main initiators of the August 1st Nanchang Uprising, and the main leader of the Red Fourth Army of the Communist Party of China. After He was overthrown by forged Comintern Telegrams and lost his power. He once experienced twists and turns. Later, he moved to Hong Kong and Canada to complete his work "My Memories", which provided important historical materials.

His wife, Ms. Yang Zilie was the first woman minister of the Communist Party of China and the first president of the Chinese women's Federation.

This book narrates all their life of Zhang Guotao and his wife. The author takes you on a long journey across mountains and rivers, looking for the tomb of Zhang Guotao and his wife.

Chapter 1 - From Peking UT to Soviet Area

Zhang Guotao' style name was Kaiyin, also known as Teli, the Russian name was Амосов (Amosov) On the Gregorian calendar on November 14, 1897 (October 20 in the Guangxu Dingyou Year of Qing Dynasty), he was born in a new official gentry family in Shanming village, Jinshan Township, Shangli District, Pingxiang County, Jiangxi Province (now Jinshan town, Shangli County, Pingxiang City) In the early Qing Dynasty, the Zhang family moved from Guangxi to Shangli. With the local natural advantages and thrifty and smart way of running a family, they gradually developed. By the generation of Zhang Guotao's grandfather, they had become local a large and prosperous family with a large number of people, good financial management and rich wealth. Zhang Guotao's father was born in 1875, his name was Jinguang, style name was Pengxiao. He was an officer in the late Qing Dynasty and the first judge trained by a political and law school in the late Qing Dynasty. He once served as a judge in the trial court of Zhejiang Province. At that time, he was

the magistrate of Xiangshan County in Zhejiang Province. He ran a bank while serving as an official. Zhang family had a rich life and a distinguished family. Zhang Guotao's mother was the second daughter of Liu Tingji, Wenjia town, Liuyang County, Hunan Province. She was born in 1866 and had two daughters and four sons. Zhang Guotao was the eldest son of his family.

Shangli County is located in the west of Jiangxi Province, in the north of Pingxiang City, in the middle of the Luoxiao mountain range, about 40 kilometers away from Pingxiang City. To the East is Yichun City and Luxi County of Jiangxi Province; to the south is connected with Anyuan Economic Development Zone and Heyao town of Xiangdong district; to the west is connected with Pukou and Fuli towns of Liling City, Hunan Province; to the north is connected with Dayao and Wenjia towns of Liuyang City. The whole county is 45 kilometers long from south to north, 25 kilometers wide from east to west, with a total area of 720.91 square kilometers. There are more than 10 kinds of minerals, such as coal, lead and porcelain clay, which produce fireworks, firecrackers, coal, building materials, food, ceramics and machinery. The local mining, paper-making and cloth weaving industries are relatively developed. Shangli is a prosperous trade center because it is located in the border area of Hunan and Jiangxi. The rolling and winding mountains provide rich natural resources for local residents. Shangli County is the hometown of fireworks and firecrackers in China. Here were born Liu Fenggao, the Minister of the military affairs of the Qing Dynasty, Yu Zenggao, the editor of Hanlin academy, Peng Hanlin, the supervisor of the imperial history, Li Youtang, the historian, and Li Yi, the founder of firecrackers. The Zhang Guotao's former residence is located in Jimu mountain, Shanming village, Jinshan Town, 6. 5km away from national highway 319. It was built in the 59th year of Kangxi (1720) of the Qing Dynasty. It is a civil quadrangle with 48 patios, facing the East and West. The former residence of Zhang Guotao covers an area of about 26 mu, with a building area of about 6,800 square meters. There are 108 rooms and 48 patios in total. The layout is compact, and the gate building is flat and wide. It is a typical enclosure form. The whole building is a single storey tile house, with the atrium as the main axis to develop on both sides. Due to the large depth of the atrium, in order to solve the problem of lighting, there are more than 40 square meters of lighting patio in the middle.

China's feudal society extended to the end of the 19th century, and it had reached the point of decline. Since the British Invaders opened China's door with gunboats in 1840, the imperialist powers have been seizing various privileges and interests of China, controlling China's financial and economic lifeline, and controlling China's political and military power. The corrupt Qing Dynasty was unable to resist the aggression of the foreign powers, but it was ruthless in exploiting the working people and suppressing the revolt of the people. The Qing Dynasty Empire has declined, and China's new bourgeoisie has ascended the stage of history. In 1905, Dr. Sun Yat-sen, the forerunner of the Chinese revolution, founded the China League in Japan. He advocated the revolutionary program of "expelling Tartars, restoring China, establishing the Republic of China, and averaging land rights", and organized the revolutionary struggle against the Qing Dynasty. Since then, new changes have taken place in China's destiny. Zhang Guotao's youth had been just in this period of great historical turning point when the Qing Dynasty went to the end and the Republic of China was founded. The society was in turmoil, and people's minds change.

In 1908, Zhang Guotao came to Pingxiang County primary school to study. Although this primary school was established after the abolition of the imperial examination, the school's host was a famous local old Confucian. He pays attention to reading scriptures and opposes new things. He calls all knowledge except scriptures "heresy" and forbids students to contact with it. But after all, history has entered the 20th century. The thought of keeping the old and not striving for progress was losing its position in the past. Chinese and Western cultures were colliding. The new and old ideas were fighting each other. Students were no longer willing to be "upright people" who follow the rules and aspire to a new life. In this way, in the collision of new and old things, Zhang Guotao spent his primary school time.

In 1911, China broke out the Xinhai Revolution, aiming at overthrowing the reactionary rule of the Qing Dynasty. After the Wuchang Uprising, the struggles all over the country surged, forming a strong flood that broke down the Qing Dynasty. Under the impact of this flood, the Qing Dynasty finally collapsed. Since then, the feudal monarchy, which lasted for more than 2,000 years in China, had come to an end. Sun Yat-sen established the Republic of China in Nanjing. The five-color national flag, representing the Han, Manchu and Mongol, was flying high over China. This revolution had effectively promoted the awakening of the national consciousness of the Chinese people and the upsurge of the demand for democracy and freedom. Men began to cut braids, women began to let go of their tangled feet, lower officials no longer worship on bended knees to their superiors. A new ethos had emerged and spread in all aspects of social life, and people's thoughts gradually tend to freedom from imprisonment.

In 1912, Zhang Guotao came to Pingxiang county secondary school that transformed from county primary school, to continue his study. When he was in middle school, Zhang Guotao had a conflict between the two wishes of "pursuing scientific knowledge" and "being enthusiastic about state affairs." At last, the latter had an advantage and he became a fanatical patriot. Zhang Jinguang, the father of Zhang Guotao, was also an old Confucian who accepted the Western way of life, but he did not take the new ideas advocated by Zhang Guotao seriously. It wasn't until Zhang Guotao proposed to cancel the engagement that Zhang Jinyu realized that his eldest son had been deeply influenced by the new thought. Zhang Guotao's grandfather once gave him a baby marriage. At Zhang Guotao's insistence, the Zhang family withdrew the marriage. Zhang Guotao was the eldest son of his family. His father had high hopes for him. Zhang's father and son often had ideological exchanges, including the collision of new and old ideas.

In October 1916, Zhang Guotao was admitted to Peking University, which became the starting point of his revolution. From then on, the young man who grew up under the impact of new and old culture began his ups and downs of life journey.

Peking University was founded in 1898 during the Wuxu Reform Movement. It was known as the "the Imperial University of Peking". It was the first official university in China, located an old mansion in the Neima Temple of Di'anmen Hejia Princess. In October 1916, when Zhang Guotao entered the University, there was a liberal art, science, law and Engineering Department and had a preparatory course, three years

Former residence of Zhang Guotao

of schooling. After graduation, you could directly enter the undergraduate course. At that time, the school had more than 1500 students from all over the country, most of them rich children. Zhang Guotao was a student of the third class in the preparatory grade of science and engineering. At that time, although the Republic of China was founded, schools around the country also showed the atmosphere of innovation, but this university, which was located in the capital city to train Beijing officials, was still conservative, lifeless and bureaucratic, it's like the atmosphere of the revolution never came here. At that time, Peking University was a place of serious corruption, the old students became popular with theatres and brothels.But not long after that, the phenomenon was gone.

The change in Peking University came after Cai Yuanpei became president. In January 1917, Cai Yuanpei, a famous educator in modern Chinese history, came to Peking University as president. At the beginning of his term in office, the great general of the academic circle with the spirit of revolutions announced publicly that "university students should take academic research as their bounden duty, and should not take university as the ladder of promotion and wealth." A few words changed the history of Peking University and the fate of Zhang Guotao. Cai Yuanpei advocated freedom of thought, academic research and discussion, and "inclusiveness". With these measures, Peking University has taken on a new look. Various political organizations of academic groups had sprung up. A new atmosphere of caring about current affairs, focusing on practical research and freely debating academic issues had begun to form among teachers and students. Cai Yuanpei invited Chen Duxiu as the dean of liberal arts of Peking University, and Chen's new youth monthly magazine moved to Peking University campus. In 1917, Hu Shi and Chen Duxiu launched the "New Culture Movement" through "New Youth". Their articles, like a stone, fell into the placid lake, causing repercussions in Peking University and even the whole country. The debate between the old and the new literature on the campus of Peking University was becoming more and more fierce. The students were gradually divided into three groups: the conservative, the middle and the radical. Zhang Guotao unconditionally approved the new trend of thought and supported vernacular writing. During his schooling at Peking University, Zhang Guotao often sent his father progressive books and periodicals such as new youth. As a keen fan of new youth, Zhang Guotao often argued with his father in his letter. In the summer vacation of 1917, 19-year-old Zhang Guotao lived in Shanghai with several revolutionaries. Zhang Guotao's eloquence was very good. Peking University, he actively participated in the student movement and carried out revolutionary propaganda everywhere. For his eloquence, later the old man of the Red Fourth Army recalled: "Chairman Zhang's mobilization before the war was the best, and every commander and fighter listened to it with enthusiasm and high morale."

Just like most young people of his time, Zhang Guotao, inspired by the new youth and the new cultural movement, paid more attention to current affairs and the future and destiny of the motherland. In addition to his lessons, he hungrily seeks new knowledge and ideas and enriches his knowledge and political literacy. Inspired by these new ideas, he began to comment on the domestic and foreign policies of the Beiyang government. On May 7, 1918, several students studying in Japan came to Peking University to join in a series and launched a struggle of learning and sports. They protested against the agreement between China and Japan on defense enemies signed by the Tokyo Conference of China and Japan. Zhang Guotao took part in the protest. On May 21, more than 1, 000 students representatives filed a petition to the presidential palace. The petition had no speeches, no slogans, and the public had no idea what the students were doing. Zhang Guotao later concluded that the parade was "too tasteless". But he also said the march was a preview of the May 4th movement. The student representatives who took part in the March then set up the Beijing student Salvation Association, and established the Nation and People magazine in the name of the National Salvation Association.

In 1919, the unfavorable voice to China at the Paris peace conference was introduced to Peking University. On May 2 of the same year, at the regular meeting of the Nation and People magazine, more than a dozen members came to talk about publishing affairs, coincidentally talking about the humiliation China would suffer in Versailles. Zhang Guotao first proposed to gather students from all schools in Beijing to hold a demonstration and the proposal was approved. On May 3, in the auditorium of the third courtyard of Peking University, Zhang Guotao was the first to give a speech to the representatives of 13 schools in Beijing.

It was the May 4th movement that really puts Zhang Guotao on the stage of history. When the May 4th Movement broke out, Zhang Guotao was the head of the speech Department of the Beijing student union. The speech department was a place where activists from all schools gathered, with a large number of people. There were more than 800 in Peking University alone. Zhang Guotao organized several speech groups and speech teams to give speeches in the open air in the streets, railway stations, market towns and other places inside and outside Beijing, distributed and posted propaganda materials, publicized the boycott of Japanese goods and exposed the Beijing government and pro-Japanese groups. The May 4th movement lasted nearly two months.

On June 2, Zhang Guotao and six other students from Peking University took to the streets to give a speech in the name of selling domestic products, but they were arrested by the police, which pushed the May 4th movement to a climax. In the next few days, warlords arrested a large number of students who gave speeches on the streets. They had to take advantage of the buildings of Peking University Law and science to imprison students. However, with the large-scale strikes of students, businessmen and workers, the Beiyang government had to make concessions.

In the event from a parade that eventually turned into a beat up traitors, Zhang Guotao always rushed ahead and became the first group of student leaders to be arrested. On June 7, at the gate of Peking University, all the students warmly welcomed Zhang Guotao and others out of prison. Zhang Guotao and others were sent back to the school by car. Zhang Guotao walked in front of the line, holding his head high, like a hero triumphant from the front. Since then, he had been elected deputy director of the Student Affairs Committee of Peking University. After the May 4th movement, Deng Zhongxia, a student of Peking University, called Zhang Guotao "an important person in students". Chang Guotao had fallen behind in his studies because of this.

In the middle of June, all China Federation of learning was established in Shanghai. Zhang Guotao, as a representative of the Beijing Federation of learning, went to Shanghai to attend the conference. He was elected to be responsible for comprehensive affairs. At this time, Chen Duxiu, who was known as the commander in chief of the May 4th movement, and 11 important leaders of the Beijing Students Federation were arrested by the Beijing government. When the news reached Shanghai, Beijing student representatives in Shanghai decided to send Zhang Guotao back to Beijing immediately to organize rescue work. At that time, there was no leader in the Beijing Federation of learning, and Zhang Guotao was immediately promoted as director-general. Zhang Guotao was very satisfied with this position, had a sense of achievement, and works very actively. He hasn't not only presided over the meeting, guided the internal work, but also was in charge of external communication, communicating with students' opinions and so on. He later wrote in his memoir: "I am too busy to go back to my bedroom for a month. When I am tired, I will lie on the couch in the office for a while and eat in the office. I worked 16 hours a day."

During his stay in Peking University, Zhang Guotao began in-depth contact with Marxism from Li Dazhao there. Intellectuals looking for new ways saw the October Revolution in Russia, where they regarded the socialist revolution as a new way to save the country and the people. Li Dazhao didn't publicize Marxism to him at the beginning, but the starting point of their discussion was the way to save the country, and they think there's no other way than to  follow the example of the Soviet Union. They confirmed that Russia's ability to overthrow the Tsar and the powerful old forces and resist external oppression from all sides was due to the leadership of the Communist Party of Russia. In other words, Marxism shines brightly.

After the May 4th movement, Zhang Guotao became the "Eye nail" of warlords. At the suggestion of Li Dazhao, Zhang Guotao took refuge in the south. He found Chen Duxiu in Shanghai and talked freely about the ideal of saving the country. Chen Duxiu told him that the main task now was not to study Marx but to establish the Communist Party of China. In Shanghai, Zhang Guotao and Chen Duxiu talked about many specific issues such as the party outline and the party constitution. Zhang Guotao hoped to launch with Li Dazhao in the north as soon as possible, organize the Beijing Group of the Communist Party of China first, and then develop to the surrounding cities.

That year Zhang Guotao's father visited his son in Beijing. Zhang's father lived in Beijing for a while and left Beijing. Zhang Guotao sent him to the station and sincerely said: "You used to be cautious, but I swore to declare war with the old society. For the convenience of your life, you can take the approach of not being jointly and severally liable for my actions. " After listening to these words, Zhang's father was a little sad and kept silent. So the father and son said goodbye.

In December 1919, on cold noon, Zhang Guotao was cooking in Xiyuan, when he saw several policemen running straight to his room. At the suggestion of his classmates, he knew that there was going to be a disaster. In a hurry, he grabbed some charcoal ashes and put them on his face. Then he continued to cook as if nothing had happened. After the police searched and tossed the battle in the room, they found nothing and went away disappointed.

Zhang Guotao and others analyzed that the search might be a revenge on the student movement. As an active member of the student movement, Zhang Guotao was naturally becoming the target of arrest. In order to avoid the arrest of the police, Zhang Guotao had to give up his desire to continue studying, and in the name of the representative of the Beijing student union, he left Beijing again and fled to Shanghai.

In August 1920, Zhang Guotao returned to Beijing to report to Li Dazhao. Li Dazhao and Zhang Shenfu established the Beijing Communist Party group basis on the Marxist Theory Research Association, and Zhang Guotao participated in the work of the establishment of the Communist Group in Beijing. Introduced by the two of them, Zhang Guotao became the third member in Beijing, responsible for organizing and communicating, and guiding the workers' movement. After the establishment of the Beijing Party Group, it had done two major tasks. First, the establishment of the Socialist Youth League of Peking University. This was an organization modeled on the Soviet Union's Communist Youth League established among young people. At that time, the Youth League had no age limit. The second was to go to Changxindian to organize the labor cram school. Zhang Guotao used his eloquence to publicize among the workers how capitalists exploited them. Li Dazhao takes 80 yuan out of his 140 yuan salary every month as the activity funds of Beijing Branch. Under his leadership, the work of the Communist Party of Beijing had been carried out in an impressive way, the most remarkable of which was the Changxindian workers' movement led by Zhang Guotao. Changxindian was 21 kilometers away from Beijing city. The repair shop of the north section of the Beijing Han railway was located here, with more than 3,000 workers. After investigation, Zhang Guotao decided to establish a labor cram school in Changxindian to educate workers and their children, which was the best way to launch the workers' movement. Zhang Guotao would not open his mouth to Li Dazhao any more for money, so he donated all the living expenses of 300 yuan a year sent to him by his family. All the comrades in the branch tried their best to donate money. Since then, this system had gradually been followed and eventually become a source of the Chinese Communist Party membership dues. Zhang Guotao, Deng Zhongxia, Zhang Tailei and others took the train to Changxindian, and mobilized workers and children to sign up for the cram school. Zhang Guotao's eloquence was outstanding and his speech was warmly welcomed by the workers. In the early days of the school, Zhang Guotao, Deng Zhongxia and Luo Zhanglong took turns as teachers, and Li Dazhao also lectured at the school. Zhang Guotao often took the place of Li Dazhao to receive the teachers and students who came to borrow books and magazines and debate.

During the period from the founding of the Beijing party organization of the First National Congress of the Communist Party of China, Zhang Guotao made great achievements both in studying Marxist theory and in initiating and organizing the

work of workers. He later became an important leader of the party and one of the leaders of the workers' movement, which had a lot to do with his experience. This was a very important first step in Zhang Guotao's political career.

According to the sugges tions of the representatives of the Communist Interna tional, Li Da respectively wrote letters to discuss with Chen Duxiu in Guangzhou and Li Dazhao in Beijing, and decided to hold the formal founding conference of the Communist Party of China in Shanghai in July, requiring two representatives from all over the country to attend the meeting in Shanghai.

Li Dazhao, as one of the founders of the Communist Party of China, was unable to attend the founding conference of the epoch-making party due to his busy official duties, Another sponsor Chen Duxiu also because presided over the work of the Board of Education in Guangdong, and was noticed by the Shanghai concession and unable to attend. Since neither Mr. Li or Mr. Chen was able to attend the conference, the preparatory work for the conference fell to the representatives of Shanghai and Beijing. Li Da and Li Hanjun participated in the preparatory work in Shanghai. In Beijing, because Liu Renjing first went to attend the meeting of the Young Chinese Society held in Nanjing, Zhang Guotao came to Shanghai ahead of time, and worked with Li Da and Li Hanjun to prepare for the first National Congress of the Communist Party of China.

July 23, 1921, at more than 8 p.m., at 106 Wangzhi Road, Shanghai, China's largest industrial center and the Workers' Sports Center, 15 people with different accents were gathered at a table. At this time, one of the young people stood up, looked around at all of you, and announced solemnly, "the founding conference of the Communist Party of China officially begins." This was Zhang Guotao, chairman of the conference. He was 24 years old at that time.

Shortly after the meeting, a middle-aged man suddenly broke into the Li Hanjun's house and opened the curtain to look around the people in the room. The stranger's sudden appearance aroused everyone's vigilance. He was immediately asked what he came here to do. The visitor vaguely replied that he wanted to find president Wang of the social Federation. Then he said that he had found the wrong place. He apologized and hurried out. There was a social union near here, but there was no chairman of the organization and no one surnamed Wang.

Li Hanjun's house was borrowed for a meeting, which attracted the attention of French concession. Later, Zhang Guotao said, "at that time, our concept of confidentiality was very weak. Maybe when the conference was held in the women's School of Bowen, the police already had noticed. When the meeting was changed in Li's house, they also didn't escape away from their attention, so they were likely to have a catch-all plans, chose to start when Marin and nickels participated."

In order to ensure the continuation of the general assembly and the safety of the delegates, Li Da and his wife suggested that the delegates leave Shanghai and go to Jiaxing Nanhu, Zhejiang Province, not far from Shanghai, to rent a cruise ship to continue the meeting. Everyone thought it was a good idea, so they left Shanghai for Jiaxing. The Congress decided that the leading organs of the central government should be called the "Central Bureau". Chen Duxiu was elected as the general secretary, Zhang Guotao was in charge of the organization, and Li Da was in charge of the publicity.

On the evening of August 5, a deep and powerful slogan sounded on the water of South Lake in the dusk: "long live the Communist Party!" "Long live the third international!" "Long live communism--the liberator of mankind!" The first Congress of the Communist Party of China closed.

After the first National Congress of the Communist Party of China, Shanghai sets up the Secretary Department of China's Labor Association, which was an open general organ of the workers' movement. Its director was Zhang Guotao, and its office was located at No. 6, Yuyangli, French concession. This was the leading body of the famous British and American tobacco factory strike in Shanghai. At that time, there was a conflict between workers and supervisors, and there were more than ten thousand strikers. Then the party headquarters of all provinces were set up to lead the workers' struggle. But this headquarters in Shanghai, in operation for about a year, was seized by the authorities.

In 1922, as the leader of the Communist Party of China, Zhang Guotao took a delegation to the Soviet Union to attend the Far East National Conference

In April 1923, Zhang Guotao (fourth from left), who went to the Soviet Union at home

held by Lenin. The meeting was against aimed at the Washington divide up the interests of the Far East. Lenin received Chang Guotao during his illness. At this meeting, in addition to the representatives of the two parties of the Kuomintang and the Communist Party, there were representatives of progressive groups and other groups.

After returning to Beijing, Zhang Guotao, who had already delayed a semester's course, received preferential treatment from Peking University and relevant professors, and passed some subjects in good faith. Under the guidance of Li Dazhao, Zhang Guotao read a lot of books introducing Marxism. After exile and loss he regained confidence and formally stepped on the political stage.

In June 1923, at the third National Congress of the Communist Party of China, he was criticized for "left-leaning" because he opposed cooperation with the Kuomintang. In February 1924, Zhang Guotao married Yang Zhilie. At that time, Zhang Guotao was 27 years old and Yang Zilie was 22 years old. On May 11, 1924, Zhang Guotao and his newly married wife Yang Zilie were arrested by the direct warlord government in Beijing. Zhang Guotao has an arrest list of more than 100 people in his hand. Because of the urgency of time, there were documents to be burned in the future. He was not tortured but was forced to press the hand model by warlords. In October 1924, Feng Yuxiang launched the "Beijing coup". On October 25, 1924, Zhang Guotao and his wife ended their iron window career for more than five months. After

11

being released from prison, he returned to the CPC Central Committee and continued to hold important positions. In January 1925, the Fourth National Congress of the Communist Party of China was a member of the Executive Committee of the Central Committee and the director of the Ministry of agriculture and industry on the Central Committee. Participate in and lead the May 30 movement.

In April 1927, Zhang Guotao, the Fifth National Congress of the Communist Party of China, was elected as a member of the Central Committee and a member of the Standing Committee of the Political Bureau of the Central Committee. In July 1927, he was a member and head of the Standing Committee of the provisional Political Bureau of the Central Committee. In 1927, he was a member of the provisional Political Bureau of the Central Committee. In June 1928, he was a member of the Political Bureau of the CPC Central Committee and went to the Soviet Union with Qu Qiubai as a delegation of the CPC to the Comintern.

In the summer of 1927, when the president of Sun Yat-sen University in Moscow, Lardik, was removed from his post due to the problem of Trotskyist, Setnikov, Secretary of the Party branch of Sun Yat-sen University, and Agur, acting president, had different opinions on the work of the school, and had serious differences in the understanding of any problems. They also had a group of supporters, formed two factions of "party affairs" and "academic". Before long, vice-chancellor Pavel Alexandrovich Myth used the contradictions between the two factions, and through joint planning with Wang Ming, he defeated Agur, and Myth was officially promoted to the post of president. From then on, Wang Ming controlled the branch of Sun Yat-sen University with the support of Myth, and gradually formed Wang Ming sectarian dogma Group with Myth as the backing and Wang Ming as the representative. This group was starting from dogmatism, which was divorced from reality and imitates the same pattern, the group was self-righteous, pretentious, self-employed, and had a sectarian position of forming a party for self-interest and eliminating dissidents, and was accustomed to the means of "cruel struggle and merciless attack". In several tides, Zhang Guotao was targeted at the head of the struggle, which made him suffer a lot.

In June 1928, Zhang Guotao went to the former Soviet Union to participate in the Sixth National Congress of the Communist Party of China. He was elected as a member of the Political Bureau of the Central Committee at the first plenary session of the Sixth Central Committee of the Communist Party of China. After the meeting, he stayed in Moscow as a representative of the Communist Party of China to the Communist International and worked in Moscow for two years. Wang Ming was studying at Sun Yat-sen University and began to make a figure in the leadership of the party. The two people were not compatible with each other and get along very badly.

In November 1930, Zhang Guotao was forced to return home. In April 1931, the CPC Central Committee sent Zhang Guotao, Chen Changhao and Shen Zemin to the Soviet Area of Hubei, Henan and Anhui. Zhang Guotao was appointed secretary of the Central Bureau and chairman of the Military Commission of the Soviet Area of Hubei, Henan and Anhui. He served as the main leader of the Red Fourth Army led by the Communist Party of China and fully led the Hubei, Henan and Anhui Soviet areas. In November of the same year, in the Provisional Central Government of the Soviet Republic of China, he was elected vice-chairman of the central executive committee.

On June 12, 1935, at noon, the vanguard of the Red First Army and Red Fourth Army met in Jiajin Mountain. Mao Zedong and Zhang Guotao agreed to meet at the mouth of Maogong River by telegram. On his way to Lianghekou, Mao Zedong saw the slogan "waiting for 300,000 base Red Army" pasted by the Red Fourth Army. He asked the Red Army Cadres: "how do you know there are 300,000 Red Army in the base?" the red army fighters replied: " according to Chairman Zhang's formula, we can calculate it ." In the Red Fourth Army and the base areas of Sichuan and Shaanxi, the commanders called Zhang Guotao "Chairman Zhang".

Before the meeting, Zhang Guotao, Chen Changhao and Xu Xiangqian, the three giants of the Fourth Front Army of the Red Army, discussed the matter of meeting in the Red Army in the base. Chen Changhao proposed "waiting for the 300,000

On July 3, 1938, Mao Zedong and Zhang Guotao were in Yanan

base Red Army" as a slogan. "How could there be so many Reds in the base?" Xu Xiangqian thought it was impossible. "They fought all the way, and the casualties and non campaign attrition ought to be very serious. Even if there were 300,000 at the time of departure, there was not so much now. It's better to leave leeway." Chen

Changhao asked, "how much is better?" Xu couldn't answer. Zhang Guotao said: "the Red Army in the base is the elder brother. It is certain that there are five times more than us. When I said that in Maoyu Town, we have only 60,000 people. Five times is three hundred thousand. Now we have developed to eighty thousand people. They will be over four hundred thousand. Let's only mention 300,000. We already leave behind the leeway." In his memoirs, Xu Xiangqian thought that the slogan affected the relationship between the two armies later. He said: "the facts after the meeting prove that the Red Army in the base is less than 20,000, and there are no 300, 000! Our propaganda embarrassed us, which made the commanders and soldiers of the Red Fourth Army talk about it one after another. "

At 5:00 p.m. on June 25, Zhang Guotao and his party arrived at Fubian, north of Maogong. In the morning, it began to rain, the rain was getting heavier, the torrential rain covered the mountains, rivers, and houses. The leader of the base, three Li away from Fubian, waited under the tarpaulin tent beside the road. All the members of the Political Bureau lined up. They were Zhang Wentian (general leader of the party after the Zunyi Conference), Mao Zedong (standing member of the Political Bureau of the base, chairman of the Chinese Soviet base government), Zhu De (Chairman of the Central Revolutionary Military Commission), Bo Gu (former chief leader of the base), even Zhou Enlai (vice chairman of the Military Commission) and Wang Jiaxiang (director of the General Political Department of the Military Commission) who were sick were also waiting in the rain. This was the highest courtesy given to Zhang Guotao by the base, and also the highest respect given by the red front army to their friend troops who selflessly assisted them. Zhang Guotao and a group of more than ten people whipped the tall and strong horses and came at a gallop. Hearing the sound of horses' hooves, Mao Zedong and others walked out of the tent and went up in the rain. Zhang Guotao jumped off his horse, shook hands with the leaders of the base one by one, hugged each other warmly, the most common sentence was "it's been eight years." He broke up with Mao Zedong in July 1927 and Zhu De in November 1927, eight years ago. At that time, they waved goodbye, They experienced military violence and agricultural violence respectively, and then established the main Red Army respectively. After rough ups and downs, they were reunited in the poor mountains and rivers of the Chuankang gap, filled with emotion. They hugged and thumped, wet on their faces, half tears, half rain.

Subsequently, a welcoming ceremony was held. At the venue sounded loud, "the Song of Two Main Force Join Forces", Mao Zedong, Zhang Guotao hand in hand, shoulder to shoulder to the rostrum. Zhu De's first speech: "comrades, the gathering of the two main Red Armies, we are not the only ones cheering, the citizens of our country and the oppressed people of the world all celebrating and cheering! This is the success of the Anti‑Japanese agrarian revolution of all Chinese citizens and the success of the party's Lenin strategy."

Chapter 2 - Overthrown by a False TG

Lin Yuying, his pseudonym once was Zhang Hao, was Lin Biao's elder cousin, style name Zuopei, Linjiadaguan village, Huilongshan Town, Tuanfeng County, Huanggang City, Hubei Province, he was born 1897. He joined the Communist Party of China in

Lin Yuying (Zhang Hao)

1922 and went to Moscow in 1933 to participate in the work of the Communist International Chinese delegation. In November 1935, he returned to China and immediately participated in the work of the Political Bureau of the Central Committee.

Since the radio station of Shanghai Central Bureau was destroyed on the eve of the long march of the Red Army in June 1934, the CPC had been disconnected from the Comintern. When Zhang Hao left Moscow in July 1935, the Red Army and the Fourth Front Army of the Communist Party of China had not split.

Mao Zedong wanted to take advantage of the prestige of the Party Central Committee to control Zhang Guotao and his 80,000 troops, but unexpectedly, Mao lost one-third of his troops. The Grassland fragmentation between Mao Zedong and Zhang Guotao was a duel between 7,000 with 80,000 people. What Mao Zedong lost was not only the army but also the people's hearts.

To recover the lost people's hearts, Mao Zedong had to fight with Zhang Guotao, Mao Zedong colluded with Zhang Hao to fake the "instructions of the Communist International". This was the biggest gamble in Mao Zedong's political career.

On December 22, 1935, Zhang Hao sent the first telegram to Zhang Guotao. As a test, Zhang Hao agreed to Zhang Guotao's proposal to hold the Seventh National Congress of the Communist Party of China, and suggested that the differences between the first and fourth front armies would be submitted to the Comintern or the Seventh National Congress of the Communist Party of China for adjudication. In this telegram, Zhang Hao did not speak on behalf of the Communist International, but communicated with Zhang Guotao in his personal capacity:

I have only two opinions at present. Please pay attention.

First, the debate within the party shouldn't be too intense;

Second, the Communist International think can organize the Northern Bureau, Shanghai Bureau, Guangzhou Bureau, Manchu Bureau, Northwest Bureau, Southwest Bureau of the CPC Central Committee, etc. according to various relations, some directly under the Central Committee, some can be managed by the delegation of the CPC to Moscow, or this is a method to unify the whole party at present. I hope this opinion can be you well thought over!

In order to cooperate with Zhang Hao, Mao Zedong called Zhu De on January 1, 1936: "our office has contacted not only the Northern Bureau and Shanghai Bureau but also the International Bureau, which is a great victory. Your development policy of the brotherhood must be reported to the Central Committee for approval at any time. That is to say, the past disputes within the party can be solved by the international and the Seventh National Congress, but the organization cannot go beyond the track, leading to self-abandonment by the party." Later, it was verified that these were untrue words.

Considering that the "Handed over to the Communist International or the Seventh National Congress of the Communist Party of China make a ruling" might be a way to solve the differences between the two armies, Zhang Guotao accepted Zhang Hao's proposal and said in the reply telegram on January 6 of the following year, "all are subject to the instructions of the Communist International."

Knowing Zhang Guotao's attitude, on January 16, 1936, under Mao Zedong's instruction, Zhang Hao sent a second telegram to Zhang Guotao in the name of international representative:

The Communist International sent me to solve the problems of the Red First Army and the Red Fourth Army. I have met Comrade Mao Zedong and learned that there is little contact with the Red First Army and the Red Fourth Army. The Communist International hopes to establish a direct relationship with the Red First Army and the Red Third Army. I have a password to contact the Comintern, if you have a message to the Comintern, I can forward it. In addition, I have participated in the Seventh World Congress and have detailed new opinions on China. I am ready to convey what I know to you.

The truth was that the Comintern did not send Zhang Hao to solve the problems of the first and fourth front armies, because the Comintern did not know that there were problems in the first and fourth front armies at all; Zhang Hao was not the authorized representative of the Comintern, but just a messenger, responsible for the restoration of the international and the CPC's Telecommunications Union. When Pan Han arrived in Yan'an in August 1936, he told Zhang Wentian, "I doubt Zhang Hao's identity as a representative of the Communist International." When Mao learned that, he was dissatisfied with Pan's "straightforwardness".

On January 20, 1936, Zhang Guotao sent a telegram to question Zhang Hao: "are you allowed to call freely? Why not report the international resolution directly? "

Since he was unable to answer Zhang Guotao's queries, Zhang Hao did not do it for the third time and kept on calling Zhang Guotao and Zhu De on January 24, 1936

A. The Comintern fully agrees with the political line of the CPC Central Committee, and believes that the Chinese party ranks first in the ranks of the Comintern, except for the United Communist Party. The Chinese revolution has become a great factor in the world revolution. The Chinese Red Army has a high position in the world. The long march of the Central Red Army is a victory.

B. The Southwest Bureau can be set up by your brother, directly under the delegation. You and other disputes on the principle of the Central Committee can be submitted for international settlement.

At this time, Zhang Hao was desperate, regardless of the consequences: "the Comintern fully agreed with the political line of the CPC Central Committee." The Communist International does not know the political line of the Central Committee of Northern Shaanxi at all. How could it "fully agree"? "The long march of the Central Red Army is a victory.". When Red First Army arrived in Northern Shaanxi, its number was less than 4,000. If this was called "victory", what were 80,000 officers and soldiers of the four front army? "The Southwest Bureau and the delegation directly under it can be set up by your office." That was to say, Zhang Hao directly belongs to Zhang Hao, and who does Zhang Hao belong to? Directly under Mao Zedong.

Mao Zedong's victory over Zhang Guotao depended not on the party or the gun, but on fake telegrams.

The above three telegrams of "false purport" were signed by Zhang Hao alone. Mao Zedong, Zhang Wentian and others did not cosign. In the future, the name of Zhang Hao (Lin Yuying) would be put first in all the telegrams between the two sides. At this time, Zhang Hao seemed to be a "supreme emperor" who was appointed by the Communist International to "solve the problems of the first and fourth front armies".

Zhang Guotao was not satisfied with Mao Zedong at that time, but he was convinced by the Communist International. Mao knew that Stalin liked the strong: to get the support of the Communist International, He ought to control the Red Army. As for how to control, the means were not important. For example, Li De's task was to send money to the Communist Party of China, and later he could become the emperor. Why can't Zhang Hao send dozens of telegrams on behalf of the Communist International? Anyway, there were so many telegrams between the two sides. Who could tell right from wrong? Who was qualified to go to the Comintern for verification?

Every telegram Mao Zedong sent to Zhang Guotao in the name of Zhang Hao was carefully deliberated. If Zhang didn't want to go north, Mao would be hard to get, saying that it was the best policy to go north, but he could go south or develop on the spot. When Zhang was afraid of calculating the old account, Mao promised "no need to talk about the differences in the past.". Knowing that Zhang intended to move westward, Mao pushed the boat along the river and said, "when Yu Ying started, comrade Stalin agreed that the main Red Army could develop in the northwest and North, and was not opposed to approaching the Soviet Union." Mao even agreed with the Zhu De's suggestion that the two central authorities suspend their functions and powers, and Lin Yuying should be the contact person on both sides. In a word, at all costs, Zhang Guotao was induced to cancel the "second Central Committee" and listen to the dispatch of the "Communist International".

The effect of Zhang Hao's false mission exceeded Mao Zedong's expectation. In terms of number and momentum, Zhang Guotao's Central Committee was far superior to that of Northern Shaanxi. After Zhang Hao called, Zhang "urgently sought unity" and agreed to Zhu De's compromise plan. On the face of it, both sides had taken a step back, which was actually good for Mao. At that time, Mao was most worried about Zhang's determination to act alone and not to accept reconciliation. In view of the great potential of the four front forces, the international community might finally recognize Zhang as the "central" fait accompli. Mao didn't expect that the " Communist International edict" had such great power. Zhang not only canceled the " second Central Committee", but also went to the north with tears in his eyes, ready to be expelled from the party and engaged in military law. After Zhang arrived in Northern Shaanxi, Mao didn't fake the imperial edict again and put Zhang to death. (Even if Mao really wanted to do this, I'm afraid his "international alliance" would not agree. In the beginning, Mao persuaded them to deceive Zhang Guotao, but only for the reasons of "dissolving the division" and "unifying the Red Army". Now the goal was achieved. Guotao bows his head and feels guilty. There was no reason for them to fall behind again.) However, the later history proved that everything had its own logic. Since the sword of Shangfang had gone out of its sheath, it ought to see blood. Even if Mao didn't want to go his own way, he had no way out.

In terms of psychological quality, Mao Zedong was far superior to Zhang Guotao. Xu Xiangqian said: "Zhang Guotao is an old opportunist who has no certain principle and direction. When it comes to business, it's 'left' and 'right'. If you take a step forward, you may shiver at the back." "Zhang Hao, in particular, called to convey the instructions of the Communist International, affirmed the correctness of the Central Committee's northward March, and spoke highly of the Central Red Army's heroic Long March, which is undoubtedly a blow to Zhang Guotao's separatism. At this time, Chen Changhao also changed his attitude and said that he will obey the decision of the Communist International." There was "international" pressure on Zhang Guotao to break down without fighting.

Compared with Mao Zedong, Zhang Guotao was a scholar. The Fourth Front Army decided to go north not because Mao Zedong was right, but because of the power of the "Communist International". Zhang was born in Peking University and believed in Marx's theory of surplus-value. Mao came from the people and knew the secret of "holding the emperor to make the princes". In China's politics, the romance of the Three Kingdoms was obviously better than Das Kapital.

On May 30, 1936, on the eve of the abolition of the "second Central Committee", Zhang Guotao checked with Zhang Hao for the last time: "do you have regular power connection with the international community? How do international delegations now represent the central authorities? What are the instructions? " We did not find Zhang Hao's reply, but saw Mao Zedong's Secret telegram to Peng Dehuai on June 15, "we are on the verge of success in communication with AIA, special news." The next day, on June 16, the communication between the CPC Central Committee and the Comintern was officially opened. On July 22, Zhang Hao, Zhang Wentian, Mao Zedong, Zhou Enlai, Bogu and Peng Dehuai sent a collective telegram to Zhu De, Zhang Guotao and Ren Bishi: " international radio communication has been unblocked since June. Brother Guotao is expected to send the information and opinions of the four front armies to the world."

Basically, the signer of July 22 was Zhang Hao's insider. The purpose of power generation was to prepare for the unexpected. This telegram answered Zhang Guotao's most concerned question: " do you have regular electricity to the international community?" This was a long-term telegram, which was divided into three parts: Party A talks about the emergency situation in Northern Shaanxi, Party B talks about the bright future of the three main forces, and Party C talks about the great situation of the northwest Grand Alliance. Finally, it was mentioned in Section D that the international contact had been "unblocked". The literal meaning of "Tong Tong" could be understood as "Tong Tong" before, but it was not. The telegraph writer was cunning.

Zhang Guotao failed to see through the mystery of the word "Tongtong". After several repetitions, he finally went north. Zhang Bei was surprised that he was not punished but welcomed after the meeting. Knowing the harshness of the "Communist International" family law, Zhang had made the worst plan. On the way to the north, he cried to Chen Changhao and said, "I can't do it. When I go to northern Shaanxi, I'm going to go to jail and get rid of the party membership. The Central Committee will give Chen Changhao the job of the Red Fourth Army." According to Xu Qianqian, Chen Changhao's boycott of Zhang's plan to move westward at the Minzhou meeting, although it was the implementation of the central government's instructions, also had some intention to replace it.

After the meeting, the situation was that both sides were afraid of beating wolves with sorghum stalks. Mao Zedong caught Zhang Guotao, a big fish, in Northern Shaanxi, but there was no place to set him up: Zhang Hao told too many lies. Once the lies helped, the consequences would be unimaginable. What worries Mao even more was that Zhang Guotao had 40,000 more people. Chen Changhao, Huang Chao, and Li Te were all fanatical dogmatists. Stalin was the only one who takes the lead. If they know Zhang Hao's "false mission", they would not give up. But Mao had no choice but to push the boat along the river and agree with Zhang Guotao's plans to advance westward, so that the two armies could keep a distance and let time to solve the problem.

The collapse of the West Road Army solved a difficult problem for Mao Zedong: "no one will ask Zhang Hao about his identity as an "international representative".

In October 1935, when Zhang Guotao set up another Central Committee at Zhuomudiao meeting, the strength comparison between the first and fourth front armies was about 1:20 (40 million to 80 thousand), Mao Zedong was at an absolute disadvantage; in October 1936, when he joined forces in Nanjing, the ratio increased to 1:4 (10 thousand to 40 thousand); after the defeat of the West Road Army in March 1937, the ratio increased to 1:2 (10 thousand to 20 thousand). With the support of the two front armies and the division of the upper ranks of the four front armies, Mao had now taken control of the Red Army. It was against this background that Mao launched the campaign to purge Zhang Guotao and threw out "secret telegrams on the grass" at the top of the party, accusing Zhang of trying to seize the Central

Committee by force and making political explanations for his leaving without saying goodbye in the grass. A year later, when Zhang Guotao left, the Communist International recognized all Mao Zedong's practices in the struggle against Zhang Guotao, and Zhang Hao left.

On April 30, 1940, Lin Yuying, Mao Zedong, Zhu De and other leaders of the Communist Party of China were invited to Yan'an Youth Cultural ditch to attend the May 1 international labor day conference. After the meeting, there was a sudden cerebral hemorrhage. Because of the timely rescue, Lin Yuying was not in danger of life, but he could not stand up and work anymore.

In late February 1942, Lin Yuying ' s condition became worse and worse. On March 5, Lin Yuying called guards, secretaries, wives and others to his side with a weak voice and said, " I can ' t do it. The revolution has been like a day for 20 years. I'm deeply sorry that I didn't see the victory of the revolution. After my death, please organize me to be buried on Taohualing opposite Yangjialing, so that I can look at the Party Central Committee and Mao Zedong every day!' At 1:45 a.m. on March 6, Lin Yuying (Zhang Hao) died at Yan'an Central Hospital at the age of 45.

The dead were extremely mournful: at Mao Zedong's suggestion, the members of the Political Bureau of the CPC Central Committee in Yan'an took turns to keep vigil for three days. On March 9, Zhang Hao was buried. Mao Zedong, Zhu De, Ren Bishi and others carried his coffin to Taohualing. This was the first and last time in Mao Zedong's life to carry the coffin to someone. Later, Mao also wrote the tombstone of " Comrade Zhang Hao's tomb".

Mao Zedong also wrote for him an elegy of "loyalty to the country, though death is glorious". Mao Zedong, Zhu De, Ren Bishi, Yang Shangkun and other central leaders guarded Lin Yuying's spirit and handled his affairs. They carried the coffin and climbed up the Taohualing cemetery where Lin Yuying lay for a long time. Finally, they realized their wish to look forward to Yang Jialing and to the Party Central Committee. After the funeral, Mao Zedong told with great care: "let Comrade Zhang Hao supervise us every day."

Lin Yuying had three sons: the second one died in 1948 when he was suppressing bandits in the Northeast; the eldest one, Lin Xiaoxia, was the vice president and secretary-general of the red flag magazine of the CPC Central Committee and secretary-general of the Party committee; the third one, Lin Hanxiong, was the Minister of the Ministry of construction, and his wife, Xiang Suyun, was the early leader of the CPC and the daughter of Xiang Ying, deputy military commander and political commissar of the New Fourth Army

Since the radio station of Shanghai Central Bureau was destroyed in June 1934, the communication between the Communist International of China and the Communist International of China was interrupted. On June 16, 1936, the communication between the radio station and the Communist International was resumed. During this period, all of Zhang Hao's opinions and instructions "issued on behalf of the Communist International" belong to the embezzlement of the name and the false dissemination of the imperial edict. Zhu De, Xu Qianqian, Chen Changhao, Liu Bocheng, the former general of the Left Route Army, were cheated for life. Zhang Guotao didn't know until he died that this was a scam directed by Mao Zedong and directed by Zhang Hao.

After the collapse of the Soviet Union in 1991, it was found from all the Communist International files that Zhang Hao's identity as "representative of the Communist International" was nothing; no one sent him to solve the problems of the first and fourth front armies, and there was no communication between him and the Communist International.

Chapter 3 - After Being Overthrown

In April 1935, the Red Fourth Army under the leadership of Zhang Guotao gave up the base area of Sichuan and Shaanxi In order to cooperate with the Red First Army. In June 1935, the Red First Army (Central Red Army) and the Red Fourth Army met in the Maogong area, Sichuan Province. At that time, the Red Fourth Army had a strong strength of nearly 80,000 people, but the Red First Army after the long march of the previous stage, only less than 30,000 people remained. On June 26, after the meeting, the Lianghe kou meeting was held. Zhang Guotao replaced Zhou Enlai as the general

Zhang Guotao (first from the right) and Wang Ming, Mao Zedong etc. in Yanan

political commissar of the Red Army. Because Zhang Guotao insisted on going south while the CPC Central Committee insisted on going north, the Red First Army and the Red Fourth Army split. Mao Zedong rate the central column, which was composed of the Red First Army and the central organs, went up to the north, and Zhang Guotao led the Red Fourth Army and some of the Red First Army troops to the south for the second time.

After the meeting of Maogong, Zhang Guotao led his department to go south to Chuankang. On October 5, 1935, Zhang Guotao held a meeting of senior cadres of the Red Army (the full name of the meeting at that time was "Party Activists Meeting") in the main hall of the Ruobuluo Temple in Baisha Village of Zhuomubao (also known as "Jiaomuzu") in Sichuan Province. He announced that he would establish another Central Committee, expel Mao Zedong, Zhou Enlai, Zhang Wentian, Bogu's party membership, and At the same time, Ye Jianying, Yang Shangkun et a are wanting. The meeting was attended by 3,000 people and lasted only two to three hours. At the meeting, the first speaker was Luo Binghui, the commander of the 12th army of the Red First Army, who was a front army. Luo cited some specific examples and said very excited. Red Fourth Army comrades unheard of, could not help but be shocked. You say one, I say one, they blame and complain the central atmosphere reached a climax. After Luo's speech, Li Zhuoran and He Changgong took the stage. He Changgong shouted the slogan: "Down with Mao Zedong!"

Two months later, on December 5, Zhang Guotao sent a telegram to Mao Zedong:

A. Here already in the name of the Party Central Committee, the Central Committee of the Communist Party of China, the central government, the Central Revolutionary Military Commission, and the headquarters of the Communist Party of China has issued documents to the outside world, and have a relationship with you.

B. You shall be called the Northern Bureau of the Communist Party of China, the Shaanxi, Gansu government and the North Road Army. You shall no longer use the name of the Central Committee of the Communist Party of China.

C. The names of the Red Fist Army and the Red Fourth Army have been canceled.

D. You must report to us the situation of the Northern Bureau, the North Road Army and the political organization for approval.

The West Route Army of the Chinese workers' and peasants' Red Army refers to the 21,800 main forces of the Red Fourth Army of the Chinese workers' and peasants' Red First Army in October 1936, accounting for two-fifths of the total number of the Red Army at that time. The main purpose of the western expedition was to control the land lifeline connecting the former Soviet Union with the Hexi Corridor in Shaanxi, Gansu and Ningxia, and to open up the northwest passage of military aid from the former Soviet Union. The failure of the West Route Army had a great influence in the CPC. The power of Zhang Guotao and his supporters was severely damaged, and Zhang Guotao was completely excluded from the leadership core.

In the early stage of "Going South" was smooth, but Chiang Kai-shek, who was informed of the Red Fourth Army, had already mobilized 80 regiments of about 200,000 people in Chengdu to wait for work. Under the attack of Kuomintang aircraft and heavy artillery, Zhang Guotao's "Going South" plan was completely bankrupt. Zhang Guotao had to withdraw his troops to Ganzi in Xikang, and the Red Fourth Army, numbering 80,000, ended up with 40,000 left. He had to turn north again and reluctantly finish the second meeting between the Red First Army and the Red Fourth Army on the one hand.

The Central Red Army established and consolidated the Shaanxi-Gansu- Ningxia base area after joining the Northern Shaanxi Red Army and the Northern Shaanxi Red Army as well as the 25th army which arrived in Northern Shaanxi in advance. On June 6, 1936, Zhang Guotao formally announced the cancellation of the "second

Central Committee" and "Central Military Commission", and prepared to establish the Northwest Bureau of the Central Committee. On July 27, 1936, the Central Committee of the Communist Party of China approved the establishment of the Northwest Bureau of the Central Committee of the red second and fourth front armies. Zhang Guotao was the Secretary, and Ren Bishi was the deputy secretary. They together led the northern movement of the red second and fourth front armies. Zhang Guotao was forced to lead the Red Fourth Army to the North together with He Long, Ren Bishi's Red Second Army and some of the Red First Army's troops.

After Zhang Guotao failed to go south, he rushed out of Erlang Mountain with his team, led the Red Second Army and Red Fourth Army, and passed the grassland for the third time. In October 1936, he and the Red First Army met again in Huining, Gansu Province in the Shaanxi-Gansu- Ningxia border area. At that time, Zhang Guotao's Red Fourth Army had more than 80,000 people with excellent equipment, while Mao Zedong, Zhang Wentian and Zhou Enlai's Red First Army had less than 8,000 people with backward equipment. Mao didn't want all the Red Four Army of Zhang Guotao to enter the Northern Shaanxi Soviet area. He was worried that Zhang Guotao would with the help of the Soviet Union to launch a mutiny, reorganize the central organization by force, and seize the highest power, so he ordered the West Route Army to march westward.

The West Route Army of the Chinese workers' and peasants' Red Army refers to the 21,800 main force of the Red Fourth Army of the Chinese workers' and peasants' Red Army in October 1936, accounting for two fifths of the total number of the Red Army at that time. At that time, it was said that the purpose of the western expedition was to control the land lifeline between Shaanxi-Gansu- Ningxia and Hexi corridor connecting the former Soviet Union, open the northwest passage of the former Soviet Union's military aid, and make the northwest base more consolidated.

In October 1936, he joined forces with the Red Army in Jiangtaibao Town (now Ningxia), Jingning County, Gansu Province. After the three main forces of the red army (the Red First Army, the Red Second Army and the Red Fourth Army) joined forces, Peng Dehuai induced Zhang Guotao to break away from the large forces and only led dozens of guards to enter the base area, which relieved Zhang Guotao's command power over the Red Fourth Army. The forward command post of the Central Military Commission led by Peng Dehuai succeeded Zhang Guotao to control the red second and fourth front army. According to the order of the Central Committee, the West Route Army of the red army was composed of the main force of the Fourth Front Army and the ninth Army. Chen Changhao was appointed as the former Secretary of the West Route Army and the political commissar of the West Route Army of the Communist Party of China, and Xu Xiangqian was the commander in chief. Under the leadership of Chen Changhao and Xu Qianqian, the West Route Army was ordered to go north. First, it tried to get through the supply line from Zhongwei and Alxa to Outer Mongolia to the former Soviet Union. Then, the Central Committee of the Communist Party of China gave up the north line under the instructions of the Communist International, and turned to get through the supply line from Gansu and Xinjiang to the former Soviet Union. After being attacked by Ma Hongkui's Ning Ma army in the north, the West Road Army retreated into the Hexi Corridor, trying to open the supply line to the former Soviet Union through Gansu and Xinjiang. Because severely attacked by Ma Bufang, Ma Buqing, the warlord of Qinghai, and Ma Hongbin, the warlord of Gansu, at the same time, due to the wrong command of the Central Military Commission and the Front line headquarters of the Military Commission (commander Peng Dehuai), the West Route Army hesitated to move eastward and westward in the Hexi Corridor, and could not get rid of the passive situation of being pursued and killed. After several months of bloody fighting, the West Route Army, with nearly 30,000 people, was almost annihilated, only Li Xiannian led more than 1,000 remnant soldiers entered Xinjiang. Most of the rest were wiped out, and a few were captured or scattered. Some of the captured and scattered personnel (such as Xu Xiangqian, etc.) later fled back to northern Shaanxi.

The West Route Army fought alone, without support, and eventually failed. The failure of the West Route Army had a great influence in the CPC. The power of Zhang Guotao and his supporters was severely damaged, and Zhang Guotao was completely excluded from the leadership core. The soldiers of the west route army suffered heavy casualties in the western expedition. According to statistics, more than 7,000 people died in the battlefield; more than 9,200 people were captured, of which more than 5,600 were killed; more than 4,000 people were exiled in Gansu, Qinghai, Ningxia (including the part that escaped after being captured) or returned to their hometown in Hubei, Henan, Anhui and Sichuan through hardships; more than 4,700 people returned to the Shaanxi-Gansu- Ningxia border area after rescue by the party organization and local people (including the part that arrived in Xinjiang)

In 1990, according to his last words, According to Xu Xiangqian's last words, half of his ashes were scattered in the Qilian Mountains after his death, accompanied by the soul of the heroes of the West Route Army who died.

In the textbooks of the mainland of China, all the contents of the "history of the party" claim that the defeat of the West Road Army was due to the implementation of Zhang Guotao's line of "escapism" and "separatism". This originates from Mao Zedong's qualitative analysis: "the failure of the West Road Army is the failure of Zhang Guotao's right opportunistic escape route.."

A large number of documents and archives disclosed in recent years show that the soldiers of the West Route Army strictly follow the telegram instructions of the Central Military Commission of the Communist Party of China to direct military operations. At that time, Mao Zedong and Zhou Enlai were the core members of the CMC. The historical truth is that Mao Zedong planned the massacre of the West Road Army, killed 20,000 people of the West Road Army by the hand of warlords, and imposed the responsibility of the massacre on Zhang Guotao.

Chen Changhao stressed: "although the West Road Army has made serious strategic mistakes, it has been working under the leadership of the correct line of the CPC Central Committee and the CMC since its establishment. Although the West Road Army has failed this time and I have made a lot of personal mistakes, I still firmly believe that the soldiers of the West Road Army have been following the correct line of the Central Committee."

In recent years, with the publication of a large number of historical documents about the West Road Army, the truth of the problem of the West Road Army has become increasingly clear. Hao Chengming, a researcher of Lanzhou West Road Army Research Association, collected more than 230 telegrams about the West Road Army from the leaders of the Central Committee, the Military Commission and the Red Army before and after the main force of the Red Fourth Army crossed the Yellow River and during its western expedition, including 24 signed by Zhang Guotao. These documents show that the formation of the Western Route Army was closely related to the major strategic decision of the CPC Central Committee on " opening up the international route", and had little to do with Zhang Guotao's split route.

Among these messages, there were two telegrams signed by Zhang Guotao alone, from which we could see clearly that Zhang Guotao had always been consistent with the Party Central Committee on the issue of the West Route Army.

One was issued on January 8, 1937. At that time, the West Road Army had moved westward to Gaotai and Linze. In the course of the westward march, the enemy continued to attack, causing more losses. Therefore, the West Route Army telegraphed the Central Committee day after day to report on the difficulties encountered and proposed to return the fourth amy and the thirty-first army to the original organizational structure, so that to complete the tasks of "approaching the distant place" and "lay the great rear of anti-Japanese". Therefore, on January 7, the presidium of the CMC telegraphed the West Route Army to instruct it not to move westward for the time being and temporary rest and reorganization in the original place. And to "rely on their own unity and struggle, do not rely on any external force.". The next day, Zhang Guotao sent a telegram to the West Route Army, saying that the instructions given by the CMC to the West Route Army were always correct and that they had paid full attention to the West Route Army If because in the past that the central route was not correct, but remained skeptical about the leadership, now should not be produced. The prestige of the Party Central Committee and the Military Commission should be enhanced in the army, especially among the cadres.

In another telegram of March 4, Zhang Guotao kept the same voice with the Central Committee, criticizing the leaders of the West Route Army and saying, "it was a mistake that you telegraphed last time and said that your losses shall be borne by the CMC. I hope that you will firmly support the Central Committee and, under the leadership of the Central Committee, unite as one person to overcome difficulties and defeat the enemy. " These cables proved that Zhang Guotao had nothing to do with the tragic defeat of the West Road Army.

On November 29, 1981, Chen Yun and Li Xiannian talked about the problem of the West Road Army, pointing out: "this problem cannot be avoided. The West Route Army crossing the river was decided by the CPC Central Committee for the implementation of the Ningxia campaign plan, which could not be said to be the product of Zhang Guotao's split line. Li Xiannian pointed out in his notes on several issues in the history of the West Road Army in 1983 that "the tasks carried out by the West Road Army are determined by the central government. The West Route Army has always been under the leadership of the Central Military Commission, and important military operations have also been instructed or approved by the Central Military Commission. Therefore, the West Road Army, in accordance with the instructions of the Central Committee, established bases in the Hexi Corridor and has opened up a route to the Soviet Union, which cannot be said to be the implementation of the Zhang Guotao line."

In March 1937, Yan'an launched a large-scale campaign to critique Zhang Guotao. Countless accusations and hats were put on Zhang Guotao's head. Zhang Guotao was critiqued and struggled by Mao Zedong, Zhang Wentian, Kaifeng, etc. Zhang Guotao described his state of mind during this period: "I recall that in the past, I felt that I am not in favor of this or that policy, opposed this or that measure, and worked hard for this or that matter, which is all branches and branches. I hate struggle and power. I think it's just funny stuff. I think that everything in the world has its dark side, politics contains sin, and revolution is not necessarily holy. It is even more despicable for those who do not hesitate to abandon morality for a certain political need. I have not yet decided to break away from the circle I have created, but I have already realized the threat of the dark side, which made me realize that the basic defects of the Communist movement are too great, and that this extremely reactionary autocracy destroyed all ideals."

Once, at the "face to face" meeting with the students of the Anti-Japanese War University, some senior commanders were very dissatisfied with Zhang Guotao's attitude of understatement admitting mistakes. When General Qian Jun of Shaolin exposed his indignation, he couldn't help but go to the stage, take off his cloth shoes, and directly punched Zhang Guotao's head and face. The audience was immediately shocked. Zhang Guotao hurriedly stood up, covered his face, raised his hand, and shouted,

"I protest, I protest. I'm still a member of the Political Bureau of the Central Committee. How dare you beat me!" Afterwards, Mao Zedong went to a Zhang Guotao's residence and apologized to him. "Comrade Guotao, you have been wronged. We've heard about today's things, the assembly is not well organized, some sorry for you. How can he hit people at will, stupid! " Zhang Guotao remained angry: "If I make any mistake, comrades can criticize and help me, but he can't hit people at will. I am still a member of the Political Bureau and chairman of the border region government." "Don't put it in your mind. I'm responsible. I'm not organized well-thought- out." "I see now, that I am the fish and the prey. There are problems with it. I can have any way?" Mao Zedong also persuaded: "it's not right to beat people. We will criticize and deal with him. But, comrade Guotao, have you ever thought about it? If you fail to pass your inspect, everyone is worried, "if you know what's wrong, you can change it. There's nothing good about it." At present, we are stable. With such a home, it's time to summarize. You, me, Wentian, Enlai, Bogu, everyone's in debt, we shall have an attitude. As you said, It's only right that we have to review our political line. Otherwise, going on like this is not good for the whole Communist Party."

On September 6, 1937, the Soviet government in the former Shaanxi-Gansu-Ningxia revolutionary base officially changed its name to the Shaanxi-Gansu-Ningxia border region government, with Yan'an as its capital, Lin Boqu as its chairman and Zhang Guotao as its vice-chairman. Because of disagreements with some leaders, Zhang Guotao was later marginalized.

Mao Zedong even publicly humiliated Zhang Guotao in Yan'an. One time they went to the theatre, the performance was about the Monk Tang went to the west to learn scriptures. Mao Zedong suddenly said to a democrat nearby, "who is the most determined monk in the Tang Dynasty to learn from the west? Tang Seng. Who is the most wavering? Pig Bajie." Then he pointed to Zhang Guotao next to him and said: "he is the pig eight rings on the long march road."Zhang Guotao heared that unbearable suddenly stood up and walks out of the theater. He turns back and says, "shameless." Mao Zedong did not change his face. He heard a distinct noise. Liu Shaoqi, a tall man, rose up from his seat and chased Zhang Guotao's back and shouted, "shut up!" In the face of these humiliations, Zhang Guotao was miserable and frustrated.

Just at this time, Wang Ming, who had attacked and suppressed Zhang Guotao when in the Soviet Union, returned to Yan'an from the Soviet Union according to directive of the Comintern, just as if he were an imperial envoy and a first leader of the Communist Party of China. Zhang Guotao was repeatedly purged by Wang Ming and expressed indifference to him. However, he still cannot escape Wang Ming continue to make things difficult for him. To his surprise, Wang Ming took the initiative to come. When Wang Ming asked Zhang Guotao to speak alone, Wang Ming first told Zhang Guotao that Huang Chao and Li Te, the former generals of the Western Route Army who had been relied on by Zhang Guotao, have confessed to be Trotskyists after interrogation in Dihua of Xinjiang, had been executed secretly. Li Te was once the chief of staff of the West Route Army and Huang Chao was the political commissar of the fifth Red Army as the pioneer. Wang Ming also killed three senior generals of the Red Army, Yu Xiusong, Zhou Dawen and Dong Yixiang. They were all the same class members of the "Central Party School" when Zhang Guotao studied in Lenin college, Moscow, and the red army elite.

When Zhang Guotao heard that his most trusted red army generals had been executed and died miserably, he said sadly, "Li Te and Huang Chao are Trotskyists, and anyone can be called Trotskyists." Wang Ming quickly explained, "you are not a Trotskyist, but you are used by Trotskyites." In the face of such blatant words and reckless actions, Zhang Guotao could not bear it any longer. He strongly condemned Wang Ming killing own comrades at would in the name of Trotskyite. Wang Ming saw Zhang Guotao look angry and said, "let's talk about it another day." He left in a hurry.

The last Yan'an dialogue between Zhang Guotao and Wang Ming, make him feel that his danger was imminent. Due to the expansion of their own counterterrorism, resulting in the life and blood debts of more than 2,000 Red Army soldiers, and the internal fight with Mao Zedong, the subordinates mistakenly killed Liu Shiqi (he Zizhen's brother-in- law), Mao's brother-in- law, and formed the cause and effect. He expected that Mao would not let him go, and the catastrophe was imminent. His heart was full of fear of death, which made him determined to flee. In My Memories, he said, "I've resisted many times and suffered setbacks, which proves that I can't turn back the fury. Do I want to be like Bukharin and others did, let Stalin killed at will? Therefore, it is absolutely necessary for me to leave the Communist Party of China and Yan'an. It is also a just act that shall be taken."

At that time, Yan'an had no room for him. After being demoted, the general lost his military power. He was assigned an empty title. Where to put his face? Yan'an already had no his stage of life and he had been completely marginalized. The main force of the West Route Army led by him was almost all annihilated on the way to the west, and was dying under the butcher's knife of the strong cavalry of Ma Bufang. Some of the red army generals who escaped by chance were successively referred to as "Trotskyists" by Wang Mingcun, the representative of the Communist International, who ordered one by one to be executed and liquidated. Only a few of the remaining old ministries, such as Chen Changhao, Li Xiannian, Xu Xiangqian and Xu Shiyou, survived. Pick up the knife and sword in the same room, since all were compatriots, why should kill each other? Zhang Guotao realized that he had no right to speak, and had been forced to a dead end. Zhang Guotao described the mood at that time in My Memories: "I was silent for a long time, is it the time to vent? Clearly knowing that I cannot reason things out with them, I have absolutely no ability to reverse the situation. Do I want to hit the stone with an egg? "

After the "double Twelfth" incident in 1936, the Kuomintang and the Communist Party had established public contacts. The CPC had set up liaison offices in Xi'an, Nanjing and other places, while the Kuomintang had sent people to Yan'an, with a view to achieving further cooperation between the Kuomintang and the Communist Party. Chiang ordered Dai Li to send someone to try to contact Zhang Guotao and ask him to meet him in Wuhan. Zhang Guotao replied, "if Chairman Jiang sent a plane to pick me up, that will be considered. But first, you need to build an airport for me in Yan'an." That means Zhang had begun to waver. Zhang Guotao finally decided to flee Yan'an, among the 36 ways, the best way was to go away.

April 4, 1938 was the day when the Kuomintang and the Communist Party jointly worshiped the mausoleum of the Yellow Emperor. Zhang Guotao, as the acting chairman of the Shaanxi-Gansu- Ningxia border region government, went to attend the worship activities. Before the mausoleum of the Yellow Emperor, he met with Jiang Dingwen, the director of the Xi'an pacification Office of the Kuomintang. After the worship, Zhang Guotao told the escorts that he had something to do in Xi'an. He asked them to go back first, and then he took a guard to the KMT's car and left. At that time, in his own words, it was for the purpose of "going to the national calamity together, resisting Japan and saving the nation."

His flee related to his reputation and survival, on his own, it might indeed be the last resort. Although he honorably served as general political commissar of the red army and a generation of red heroes galloping on the battlefield, there was still a weak side of human nature, that is, death was imminent, he can't wait to die, he needed to save his life. However, his departure caused many of his Red Army subordinates to be greatly implicated later, or dismissed, or long-term censored, with a wide range of repercussions, I don't know whether it was done by heroes or not. Xin Qiji, the poet of the Song Dynasty, wrote "Bid farewell to the twelfth brother Jiamao": "The general who has experienced countless battles has lost his reputation because of his defeat. To see my friend off at the bridge by the river, and look back at my hometown thousands of miles away, and say goodbye to my old friend forever. Who will accompany me to drink in the moonlight? " This seems to have been specially written by the ancients to the present.

Zhang Guotao to Wuhan after, Zhou Enlai and others did not abandon him, repeatedly sent people to persuade him to return no results. Finally, Zhang Guotao proposed to Zhou Enlai that he wanted to see Chiang Kai Shek. On the afternoon of April 16, 1938, Zhou Enlai accompanied Zhang Guotao across the river to Wuchang to see Chiang Kai Shek. When Zhang Guotao saw Chiang Kai-shek, he was opening said, "Brother I have been confused for many years on the outside." Zhou Enlai immediately said to him, "you are confused, I am not confused." Then, in his capacity as acting chairman of the border region, Zhang Guotao reported to Chiang Kai Shek some information about the government of the border region. After returning to the office, Zhang Guotao said to Zhou that both parties of the Kuomintang and the Communist Party were now very bad, and he was willing to leave his political career temporarily--he was determined to get rid of the " monitoring" and finally leave. "This Communist Party is not the party that I have been yearning for and fighting for all my life," Zhang said in his resignation statement. Several years later, Zhou Enlai said to Zhang Guotao, "this Communist Party is founded by you. You can't leave ah!"

Later, Zhang Guotao had a tortuous experience. He once joined the Kuomintang military unification and worked under Dai Li. After the victory of the Anti-Japanese War, he once served as the director of the Jiangxi branch of the General Administration of rehabilitation and relief of the executive yuan of the Kuomintang government. From 1946 to 1948, he ran the Move Forward Creatively Newspaper in Shanghai. At the end of 1948, he and his family moved to Taipei because of the change in the political environment. In Taiwan, he was in a worse situation. Not only was he ignored, but he also could not continue to serve in the military unification, and even his favorite house was occupied. In this case, frustrated Zhang Guotao left Taipei and went to Hong Kong in the winter of 1949 with his wife Yang Zilie and three sons. Since then, he and family had lived for 16 years in Hong Kong.

After the Korean War broke out in 1950, the price of gold soared all the way. He self-confident that he had studied economics at Peking University, forgot the principle of "caution when entering the market" and started the business of " speculating gold" in the financial market. As a result, the price of gold suddenly plummeted overnight, bringing his investment down to a terrible level.

In 1961, the "celebrity center" of Kansas University in the United States found Zhang Guotao and expressed the hope that Zhang Guotao would write his memoirs for them. As a remuneration, Zhang Guotao could provide him with 2,000 Hong Kong dollars a month. Zhang Guotao agreed. Therefore, with the help of two Jiangxi compatriots, He began to collect materials such as the early days of the Communist Party of China's joint construction and brew the writing of memoirs. Five years later, Zhang Guotao's memoirs were completed. In 1966, Hong Kong's "Ming Pao Monthly" purchased the Chinese copyright, which is "My Memories". From 1966 began in the "Ming Pao" serialized, in 1971 began in the "Ming Pao Monthly" serialized, in 1974 was combined into three books publishing (Chinese version). It was said that "Ming Pao Monthly" to pay a large sum to the amount Zhang Guotao couple of contribution fees and royalties, which also became the main economic income of Zhang Guotao's family for more than ten years.

In 1966, great changes took place in the world, and a "Cultural Revolution" took place in mainland China. Zhang Guotao read newspapers every day and paid close attention to the "Cultural Revolution". He was also worried about the turmoil in the mainland, but when he thought that he was an outsider, he doesn't think much anymore. As for his personal safety, Zhang Guotao believed that Hong Kong was under British control, and that no matter how noisy the mainland was, it can't be riotous in British territory. Red guards dare not come to Hong Kong to catch themselves, he could live in Hong Kong at ease. Who would have thought that the wave of the Cultural

Revolution had spread to Hong Kong, and the Red Guard poster that hunted Zhang Guotao had been pasted all over the streets of the central and Mongkok districts, which made this enclave also stand in a state of fear, and people were in danger. People don't know what would happen tomorrow morning.

By 1967, the "Cultural Revolution" in the mainland was even more fierce. The fire of the Cultural Revolution also burned in Hong Kong, and the beating, smashing, robbing and seizing happened almost every day. One day, Zhang Guotao wandered into the street, and suddenly saw that a big poster that was posted on the street of Hong Kong. He could not help but face changed, panting to run home, told Yang Zilie this situation. Yang Zilie's mood was also tense. Since then, they had been uneasy, closed the door, no longer out of the house. During this period, Zhang Guotao read the newspaper more carefully, read some reports over and over again, and pondered the meaning between the lines.

One day, a neighbor came to tell Yang that the other day, two strangers came here to inquire about Zhang Guotao's address. Yang Zilie quickly told Zhang Guotao about this situation. The more Chang Guotao thought about it, the more uneasy it was, his address in Hong Kong was not publicized. Only a few relatives and friends know it, how could strangers come here to inquire about his address? Is it not the red guards from the mainland or any other rebel faction organizations that sent people to Hong Kong? The more he and Yang think about it, the more afraid they were. It was a surprise. Zhang Guotao couldn't sleep almost every day. He was afraid to live in war. With the developed information dissemination in those days, Zhang Guotao should know that a large number of old Red Army departments and friends, such as Liu Shaoqi, Peng Dehuai, Deng Xiaoping, Chen Changhao, Xu Qianqian and Tao Zhu, had been put in prison, or the experience of being a prisoner, once again felt that the disaster was imminent, the sense of terror of death suddenly rose, Hong Kong was no longer a safe place to stay, so the couple decided to leave after night discussion, and the whole family flew to Canada to be reunited with their son.

At that time, Zhang Haiwei, the eldest son of Zhang Guotao, taught mathematics in Toronto, Canada. Zhang Xiangchu, the second son, worked as a doctor in New York, USA. Zhang Yuchuan, the third son, worked as an engineer in Toronto, Canada. With the special approval of Zhou Enlai, Zhang Xiangchu studied medicine in Guangzhou Zhongshan Medical College in the 1950s. The three sons received doctorates and master's degrees respectively, with eight grandchildren. Mr. and Mrs. Zhang Guotao first arrived in New York and soon moved to Toronto. Zhang Guotao and his wife first lived together with the eldest son's family, but soon found that the eldest son's income was difficult to support the family, so they moved out of the son's family and lived in a nursing home. After his family moved to Canada, Zhang Guotao deliberately avoided the public's attention, faded out of the Jianghu and never made public. In his later years, Zhang Guotao loved listening to Chinese radio. When Zhang Guotao was living in poverty, Jiang Jingguo sent 10,000 US dollars to him. After Zhang died, Jiang Jingguo sent 3,500 US dollars in funeral expenses by wire transfer from the Secretary-General of the Central Committee of the Kuomintang. Through a family portrait of Zhang Guotao's family in Toronto, people could see some situations at that time.

In the photo, Zhang Guotao's clothes were straight, Yang Zilie was dressed in cheongsam, and the three generations of his ancestors and grandchildren were jubilant and happy. In 1975, Pierre Trudeau (father of Justin Trudeau, Prime Minister of Canada at the beginning of the 21st century), who was very friendly to China at that time, take advantage of meeting opportunities in Toronto, he went to visit Zhang Guotao and his wife and expressed the Canadian government's concern and respect for modern Chinese historical figures. In September 1976, Mao Zedong died. Someone told Zhang Guotao the news. Zhang Chang sighed, "Our years are dead! Like Mao Zedong, I am a man who is going to die. It is only a matter of time before I die."

In 1977, Zhang Guotao suddenly suffered a stroke and his right half was paralyzed. After the stroke, Zhang Guotao was unable to move, unable to pronounce clearly, and had little use for his ears. He could only sit in a wheelchair and move indoors every day. Before Mrs. Zhang and their friend visit, Mrs. Zhang asks their friend to write down some words or names to be talked about in big words. When talking, she would show them to him to help him hear and remember. So the friend made some preparation in advance. When their friend saw Zhang Guotao, Zhang was very happy, cheered and laughed. He held their friend's hand with his left hand which was still able to move and said, "I'm very happy to see you when I'm old and ill." His sincere feelings, overflowing with words, touched their friend very much.

On December 3, 1979, at the age of 82, Zhang Guotao died on the land far away from his hometown, and he had gone through to walk his bumpy and legendary road of life with reputation and slander interlace.

On December 5, 1979, Zhang Guotao was buried in the Pine Hills Cemetery in Toronto. In a foreign country across the sea, on the peaceful slope of Lake Ontario, Zhang Guotao finally had his own home, a pure land for him to rest and long term sleep after his death. It was fortunate for him to be able to live abroad and avoid years the domestic chaos. People can't imagine that if Zhang Guotao stayed in the mainland with humiliation, confessed his mistake with modesty, stopped fighting, and kept a low profile, people don't know if he could escape the liquidation of all previous struggles and rectification movements from inside the Communist Party? In the stormy waves of political movements after the founding of the people's Republic of China, I don't know what kind of exile and historical liquidation he would experience, could he escape the catastrophe of the "Cultural Revolution" of ten years? . Compared with the endings of Liu Shaoqi, Peng Dehuai, he long and Lin Biao, Zhang Guotao's life was undoubtedly a lot luckier.

Since the Opium War, modern China had gone through many hardships, she was trampled by the iron hoof, divided by the powers. Generation after generation of people with lofty ideals had gone on in order to save China and the people and advance wave upon wave, use their lives to spare no effort fight. After the death of Zhang Guotao, the history of modern China had turned over many chapters. Nowadays, with the vicissitudes of the world and the changes of the stars, Everything had become a thing of the past was as transient as floating clouds. Many early leaders of the Communist Party of China, such as Chen Duxiu, Wang Ming, Qu Qiubai, and Bo Gu, had been affirmed the historical merit and made a positive assessment by the new "history of the party" compiled by the Central Party School of China. This shows that the study of the official language and the history of the party began to have a new value orientation, no longer entangled in the past political grudges and feelings, no longer to judge who was the hero by success and failure. The academic community also began to evaluate the modern Chinese historical figures objectively, in order to enhance the transparency of history, which was of positive significance. Although there was a long way to go, there were still many cases that need to restore the historical truth.

Ms. Qin Qian was the president of Canadian Chinese food and Culture Association and vice president of the world China Cuisine Federation for another ten years. She had been operating the "Number One Scholar Restaurant " in Chinatown, Central Toronto since 1973, until the end of her business in 2004, This was by far the longest running Chinese restaurant in Toronto without changing its owner. In her 30 years of Chinese restaurant business, she had experienced too many events and received too many guests. However, she still remembers how many times Zhang Guotao visited the restaurant. Qin Qian recalled that around 1975, a frequent customer of the restaurant helped an elderly man to eat in the " Number One Scholar Restaurant". The old man was tall because he was old, his actions somewhat slow. When Qin Qian greeted two guests and receives them, the frequent customer introduced to say, "this is Mr. Zhang Guotao, Mr. Zhang." Qin Qian said, "at that time, I am still a young girl. I didn't know much about political

figures, and I didn't know who Zhang Guotao was. However, the further introduction of the frequent customer attracted my attention, and I knew that this is a great man." Qin also said that Mr. Zhang published his memoir. Qin Qian believes that Mr. Zhang was kind and worthy of respect old man. At that time, the "Number One Scholar Restaurant" in Toronto was the only non-Cantonese restaurant. All diners who wanted to eat northern food would come to the "Number One Scholar Restaurant". Since then, Zhang Guotao had come to the restaurant four or five times, accompanied by one or two friends each time. Zhang Guotao likes the dish of " braised lion's head". He suggested that the restaurant burns it as bad as possible. Therefore, every time Zhang Guotao came to eat, he would call in advance the restaurant. The Shandong master of the restaurant specially prepared the rotten lion's head for him. Zhang Guotao was particularly satisfied after eating. Qin Qian said that Zhang Guotao was a very kind old man. He was kind, refined, polite, slow in speech, and cultivated. He doesn't look like a reckless military man who leads the troops to fight. Later, Qin Qian bought three volumes of Zhang Guotao's "My Memories" in the Chinese bookstore in Chinatown. With respect to Mr. Zhang, she bought them without hesitation. She planed to ask Zhang Guotao to sign his name when he comes back to her restaurant again. However, Zhang Guotao was never seen again. Once she saw the frequent customer who had come to dinner with Zhang Guotao, Qin Qian asked Zhang why he didn't come again? The friend said, "Mr. Zhang died of illness."

On the other side of the ocean, in Nankan scenic spot in the south suburb of Bazhong County, Sichuan Province, China, there was a cemetery for the red army martyrs. There stands a statue of Zhang Guotao, inscribed with the inscription: " representative of the First National Congress of the Communist Party of China, general political commissar of the red army", which was located in the forest of Steles for the red army generals in the Soviet Area of Sichuan, Shaanxi, for people to pay their homage and respects.

In 2010, Shangli County Government decided to put aside the dispute and invest in repairing the former residence of Zhang Guotao and his brother Zhang Guoshu. All sectors of society around the protection of cultural relics on "whether according to the class origin and background" of a heated debate. Some people believe that historical figures, whether positive or negative, who had an impact, should be given appropriate protection of their remains, so that we could recover to the true face of history. Article 2 of the law of the people's Republic of China on the protection of cultural relics stipulates that "Important modern historical sites, objects and representative buildings related to major historical events, revolutionary movements or famous figures and of great commemorative significance, educational significance or historical value shall are protected by the state." Therefore, the former residence of Zhang Guotao should be protected, which had nothing to do with his historical behavior. Not to mention, historical behavior itself was an ideological concept with considerable flexibility.

Although Zhang Guotao's achievements and demerits in his life had been scattered like smoke and clouds, they had left us too much thinking. He was the leader of the May 4th student movement and laid the foundation for the birth of the Communist Party of China. As one of the founders, he served as the chairman of the first National Congress of the Communist Party of China and the head of the organization of the Communist Party of China. He experienced many critical moments in the early stage of the Chinese revolution and participated in many major decisions. Then he commanded the main force of the Red Army, the Long March, the army, the horse, the rush, the ups and downs. There were too many behind the scenes stories, too many In order to stand the test of history, historians need to depoliticize, open the hidden secret box, eliminate the false and reserve the true, and don't hide anything, write history truthfully, so that it could stand the test of future generations.

In the history of the modern Chinese revolution, Zhang Guotao was undoubtedly a person who had played an important role and can't bypass it. When some boycotts, grudges and love and hatred had disappeared, the kind-hearted Chinese would continue to look for the buried historical memory of the near extinction, It would take many years to digest some historical vicissitudes to interpret and recall some historical figures with goodwill.

Although Zhang Guotao died in a foreign country in his later years, he witnessed the development trajectory of the Communist Party of China and Chinese society with the eyes of a bystander. A columnist once visited Zhang Guotao in his later years, which was one of the few people who had seen Zhang in his later years. The impression of the columnist was that Zhang Guotao never spoke ill of the Communist Party and Mao Zedong and as far as possible no talk about politic topic, whether in Hong Kong or abroad.

Chapter 4-Madam Yang Zilie

Yang Zilie (December 9, 1902 -   March 27, 1994) was born in a book fragrant family in Zaoyang County, Hubei Province. In the summer of 1918, Yang Zilie study of the Hubei Provincial Women's normal school, located in the Loess Slope of Wuchang (now Shouyi Road), where he was educated by Chen Tanqiu and others. She secretly read a large number of revolutionary books and magazines, dressed in short shirts and long skirts, and gradually grew into a conscious revolutionary. One day in April 1919, at the age of 17, she read a vernacular newspaper for the first time in her life, which not only had objected to the 21 articles, but also had the fresh topics such as opposing arranged marriage, opposing women's foot-binding and breast binding, women should cut their hair, which made her feel sad, angry and happy. The students were equally excited when they read it. Along with the May 4th movement, there were parades, lectures, debates, entertainment meetings, and plays. Russell and Dewey came to Wuhan to give speeches in their schools. Liang Qichao went to Wuchang men's higher normal school to give speeches. Yang Zilie and her

classmates were also allowed to attend lectures. They release their corsets, tear off their tight vest, cut their hair. Chen Bilan (Mrs. Peng Shu), Zhuang Youyi (Mrs. Lu Chen), Xu Quanzhi (Mrs. Chen Tanqiu) and Xia Zhixu (Mrs. Zhao Shiyan) from Huangpi, Yingshan, Hanyang and Wuhan were classmates. At the same time, they were introduced by Lin Yunan and Liu Changqun, she joined the Socialist Youth League in April 1922 and the Communist Party of China in October 1922. In the autumn of 1922, Xu Quanzhi, Xia Zhixu, Yang Zilie, Chen Bilan, Zhuang Youyi, etc. set off a school tide that shocked Hubei.

On February 1923, Yang Zilie went north to continue his studies and entered Beijing Women's normal university. At the same time, she studied in an art school in

Beijing. She met Zhang Guotao in Beijing and married him in February 1924. She went to Moscow twice for further study and became an active figure in the early Chinese women's movement. Yang Zilie was the first woman minister of the CPC and the first president of all China Women's Federation.

In the spring of 1931, Zhang Guotao was sent to the base areas of Hubei, Henan and Anhui. Yang Zilie was left in Shanghai by the CPC Central Committee to work underground. After the organization of the CPC in Shanghai was destroyed by the Kuomintang in 1934, Yang Zilie lost the organization's contact. She first returned to her hometown to avoid chaos, and then returned to Shanghai to study obstetrics and gynecology. After the cooperation between the Kuomintang and the Communist Party, she was introduced by the Nanjing Eighth Route Army Office and traveled to Yan'an with her son. After Yang Zilie returned to the team, the most urgent requirement was hoping that the central organization department would restore her party status. Although Yang Zilie was an old cadre of the Communist Party of China and her husband Zhang Guotao was still a member of the Political Bureau of the Central Committee of the Communist Party of China and the acting chairman of the border region government at this time, the central organization department would investigate her performance after losing contact with the organization and test her in the work. Yang was assigned to the border region government as a political teacher, and was a volunteer obstetrician in the Central Hospital of the border region. She worked enthusiastically and was highly praised by President Fu Lianzhang. At that time, Cai Chang and her husband Li Fuchun were both working in the central organization department and participated in the review of the history of Yang Zilie after he left the party. Cai Chang and Yang Zilie were acquaintances for more than ten years and had a good understanding of Yang's past history. In June 1938, when Mao Zedong approved Yang Zilie to leave Yan'an with her son and reunite with Zhang Guotao in Wuhan, her party membership always had not been restored.

Yang recalled that when she first arrived in Yan'an, she could not see any serious conflict between Mao and Zhang. At that time, Mao invited Zhang and his wife to have a meal. Mao said, "the Kuomintang has a pair of Zhang Yang (Zhang Xueliang and Yang Hucheng), and our Communist Party also has a pair of Zhang Yang (Zhang Guotao and Yang Zilie).".

In April 1938, Zhang Guotao, then chairman of the Shaanxi-Gansu- Ningxia border region government, took the opportunity of worshiping the mausoleum of the Yellow Emperor to leave Yan'an and the Communist Party of China that he personally created in. Yang recalled that at first she thought Zhang Guotao had been ordered to go to Xi'an or other places to engage in secret work. In her heart, she blamed him for not telling himself and was embarrassed to ask anyone.

Yang Zilie recalled: "After almost a month, I didn't see Guotao coming back and he didn't have a word for me. Though I am sad in my heart, I am ashamed to ask who.

Sitting in the front row on the left is Ms Yang Zilie

I have two kinds of psychology: first, in the era of secret work, whoever is not in charge of the work will not know the secret of the work. What's more, the white terror was very serious at that time. The less the comrades know about the party ' s work secret, the better. I have developed this habit in the past ten years. Secondly, Guotao is my lover and dearest. Where did he go? He didn't tell me. If I ask someone (it's never happened before). Can anyone else tell me? It's been nearly seven years since we left. It's only a few months since we gathered, but he left without notice me. I was angry and didn't want to ask anyone."

Almost a month later, the central organization department called Yang Zilie to go there quickly. She thought it was to restore her party membership, and she was very happy. At the middle organization department, Chen Yun invited her to a room and said in a low voice, "Comrade Zilie, do you know? Recently, a great event had taken place at the party that shocked the whole party. " She expressed surprise that she did not know at all. Chen Yun frowned and bowed his head to tell her, " Guotao is gone!" Subsequently, Chen Yun gave her a letter: "Guotao has a letter for you. He is waiting for you in Hankou. Will you go?" She was full of desire to find Zhang Guotao. She wished she could see him at once. For a moment, she was embarrassed to say, "I'll think about it."

Chen Yun looks at her paunch and asks how many months she had been pregnant. She says six months. Chen Yun said with great concern, "then you will be careful! If you have comrades gossiping, you can tell me. "

Zhang Guotao's letter was very simple, to the effect that: "I love my sister, Zilie's wife: leave without saying goodbye, please forgive me. I am in Yan'an. I am waiting for you in Hankou. I hope my sister will come to Hankou with her beloved Haiwei. "

The letter was written in Xi'an at the beginning of April, which was May 16, that was to say, it had been more than a month since the letter arrived in Yan'an. All of a sudden, she found that the comrades she used to know became indifferent to her, and her former smile disappeared, She felt that the world was cool and the people were warm. The next morning she went to see Mao Zedong. Liu Shaoqi and Zhang Wentian were both there. Before she opened her mouth, those who knew her inner feelings approached her warmly, patted her gently on the shoulder, and laughed loudly as if seriously and humorously, saying, "OK, Zilie, Guotao left you and ran away!" It took her a long time to calm down and say, "why did he leave? I don't understand! I want to go to Hankou to find him, ask him clearly, and find him back. " "Good! If you can get Guotao back, you are a great hero of the Communist Party." Mao Zedong was so happy that he held out his right thumb. Liu Shaoqi said to her kindly, "Zilie, come and play with me." She recalled that Zhang Wentian was tensing a "Bolshevik" face, as if he didn't see her, holding his head up, stood up and left quietly.

After a few days, she saw Li Fuchun and formally proposed to go to Hankou to find Zhang Guotao for approval of the organization department. Li Fuchun replied, "let the central committee held a meeting to decide, and then inform you." Those days, pregnant with her worry, often do not think about food and tea, secretly tears, in front of people but also to endure tears. Finally, Li Fuchun's reply came: "the Central Committee has held a meeting. It is decided that if you don't go to Hankou, children will still be sent to Moscow to study." She could no longer hold back her tears, covering her face with her hands and crying, "no, I'm going! I'm going to Hankou to see Guotao! "

She wrote to the Central Committee that she would go back to her hometown, Hubei Province, to have children. After three or four days of silence, she went to the central organization to find Chen Yun and Li Fuchun. "Chairman Mao decided not to go at the meeting of the Central Committee," said Li Fuchun, grimacing! Organization department doesn't care. " Chen Yun asked gently: "how many months has the child been?" She said seven months ago. Chen Yun whispered, "if you want to go, go!"

Yang Zilie immediately climbed several slopes to find Mao Zedong and said, " Chairman Mao, I want to go home and raise children. Please approve me!" Mao's voice was very low: "that's the head of the organization department. You go to them." She said earnestly, "no, I just came from the Organization Department, and Comrade

Fuchun said it is up to you! You two, you push him, he pushes you! How can I do that? You see, I have a big belly. I can't run any more. Just write me a note now!" Mao Zedong, who was writing the article, wrote on the white paper, "let Comrade Zilie go home!" As he wrote, he said, "you are good, because Guotao is not good After you go to Hankou, the party can be responsible for all the expenses of having a child. You can come back to the party at any time." Mao also meaningfully asked her to tell Zhang Guotao, "we have been friends for many years, and we shall leave room for each other." She was also granted a travel fee of 500 French dollars. With this note, Yang Zilie left Yan'an with her child and sister. Finally, Yang chose to stick to her husband. For the sake of her children and the integrity and happiness of her family, she would rather leave behind all the status, power and ambition of the party, just to stay with him forever. Since then, the Zhang family had been separated from the motherland, and Guotao and Zilie, the ideal young people, had no chance to witness the prosperity of the motherland.

Mrs. Zhang, who was in a high revolutionary mood at that time, although she was old and had hurt her legs, she had to move with her staff, but she was full of spirit, had a deep Buddhist heart, and cared for her family without forgetting the state affairs. After having a buffet in the old people's hospital every day, I went to the sanatorium by streetcar to accompany Guotao, and talked with Guotao at the side of the sickbed to comfort him. It could be said that he was "the lifelong companion of a couple in need". Children and grandchildren often come to the hospital to have a good time.

Yang Zilie and Zhang Guotao love each other, live and die, and help each other for more than half a century. Yang Zilie wrote "the past is like smoke", later renamed " the Memoirs of Madame Zhang Guotao". In 1970, it was edited by the Hong Kong Center for China Studies and printed by UnionPay press. In 1994, 15 years after Zhang Guotao's death, Yang Zilie died at the age of 92, and they were buried together in the Pine Hills Cemetery in Toronto.

Chapter 5 - "My Memories" by Zhang Guotao

After Zhang Guotao and his family moved to Hong Kong in the winter of 1949, Some American Research Institute came to his door. In the eyes of these institutions, Zhang Guotao once served as a senior leader of the Communist Party of China for a long time. If he could review and summarize the history of his participation, it would have a strong research value. In 1961, researchers from the center for celebrities of Kansas University in the United States found Zhang Guotao and proposed that Zhang Guotao write memoirs for the center. In return, the celebrity Centre provides it with HK $ 2,000 a month. Zhang Guo tao began to write his memoirs. In 1966, Hong Kong's Ming Pao Monthly purchased the copyright of its memoirs and began to serialize them on the title of my memories, which was later published in a collection. Shortly after he began to write his memoirs, Zhang Guotao was noticed by

the American government. In the eyes of the U.S. government, although Zhang Guotao had long been far away from the political center, or even from politics, because of his special identity, he not only had a good understanding of the early history of the Communist Party of China, but also was very familiar with the operation of the early policies of the Communist Party of China, and he had long-term contacts with the current leaders of China, and was familiar with their personalities and ways of doing things. Therefore, Zhang Guotao proposed The information provided ways of reference values for the United States to understand the political situation in mainland China at that time.

In the mid-1960s or so, the U.S. government found Zhang Guotao and asked him to provide political analysis of current affairs on the mainland from time to time. At this time, various political forces in the world were divided and reorganized, and the situation was turbulent. Chinese society was in the period of Cultural Revolution, and political movements were rising one after another.

From 1966 to 1974, My Memories was written in three volumes, nearly a million words. It details the founding process, the development process of the Communist Party of China, and the communication between the author and the political figures of the Communist Party of China. It describes the love, hate, sorrow and joy of the Soviet Area, the vicissitudes of Yan'an, and the words and deeds of Sun Yat-sen, Jiang Jieshi, Zhang Xueliang, Chen Duxiu, Wang Ming, Qu Qiubai, Bo Gu, Li Lisan, Mao Zedong, Liu Shaoqi, Zhou Enlai, Zhu De, He Long, Peng Dehuai, etc., which were the first-hand and detailed historical materials about the history of the Communist Party of China. For the past years, the process of the struggle and conflict between the former Soviet Party and the central Republic, and the inside story of the Comintern in China, the book also details the context. Many more historical facts had been publicly declassified for the first time through this book. For example, the "reconciliation" of the Xi'an Incident did not come from the expectation of Zhang Xueliang and other officials of the central Republic at that time, nor from the military pressure of the Kuomintang. It was Stalin's instruction issued according to the situation of the Communist International at that time, and Zhou Enlai was ordered to mediate the success.

In this book, many critical moments, important occasions, before and behind the scenes of the Chinese revolution, the leaders of the Red Army and the Communist Party of China, the separation of life and death, love and hatred, ups and downs of honor and disgrace, heroic and tragic, were personally witnessed by Zhang Guotao. Through carding, he talked about the vicissitudes of life, the bleakness of history, the soul stirring, gripping.

Zhang Guotao reflected in his later years, he said that he and Mao Zedong were on the same road, knew Peking University in the May 4th period, and were all vigorous and passionate young people who fought for the faith. However, after a lot of personal experience, they all wanted to be the eldest, and one of them ought to be defeated. Xu Shiyou, general of the founding of the Communist Party of China, once said that "Apart from Chairman Mao, no one in the party is Zhang Guotao's opponent". This inference was completely in line with the situation at that time, because at that time, only Zhang Guotao could command the main force of the Red Army, maintain an army and defy orders from the central government. At that time, there were no people who one word was more prized than the sacred treasures, so the various forces of the Red Army were roughly equal. In Mao Zedong's memory, the internal struggle with Zhang Guotao was the darkest period in his life, and he himself had been ups and downs. Since there was Mao Zedong, why was there Zhang Guotao? Any version of the history of the Communist Party of China should not get around the name of Zhang Guotao.

In 1919, Zhang Guotao and Mao Zedong met for the first time in the Peking University Library. At that time, Zhang was a well-known student leader, but Mao was only an absent student and a temporary worker in the Peking University Library. Li Dazhao introduced to Mao Zedong: "this is Zhang Teli, Comrade Zhang Guotao." Mao Zedong warmly shook hands with Zhang Guotao, introduced himself and said, "I am Mao Runzhi of Hunan Province." Zhang Guotao nodded, then talked with Li Dazhao. Many years later, in an interview with snow, an American journalist in Northern Shaanxi, Mao Zedong talked about his acquaintance and said with deep feelings, "they look down upon me as a country bumpkin." From then on, Mao Zhang built a bridge.

At the first National Congress of the Communist Party of China, Chen Duxiu did not attend the meeting. The actual convener of the meeting was Zhang Guotao, and Mao attended as a member of the Socialist Youth League. At the end of the first National Congress, Chen Duxiu was elected general secretary, Li Da was Minister of propaganda, Zhang was Minister of organization, one of the top three leaders, equivalent to the member of the Standing Committee of the Political Bureau. Mao Zedong was not appointed at the first National Congress of the Communist Party of China. After the founding of the Communist Party of China, Zhang's position was above Mao Zedong's for a long time. Since then, both had served as important leaders of the Soviet Area and the Red Army. During the Long March, Mao Gong, a member of the Red Army and the Fourth Front Army in Xiaojin County, Sichuan Province, met Zhang Guotao and Mao Zedong, who openly had major political differences. Mao Zhang was not only a comrade in the party, but also a matchmaker, competing for supremacy by the deer. There were no two tigers in one mountain. At last, there will be a win.

In the ups and downs of Chinese political, ideological and cultural history in the last century, Zhang Guotao, together with his peers, Chen Duxiu, Li Dazhao, Wang Ming, Qu Qiubai, Bogu and Li Lisan, once shouldered the historical mission of salvation and enlightenment, leaving a long and complex historical picture. Chen Duxiu, with the help of Zhang Guotao, the student leader of Peking University, founded the new youth. Qu Qiubai translated the lyrics of the international song. He was the first to systematically translate Marx's literary theory and Soviet works. He was the first to introduce the new Soviet Republic to China. He was the first to try to use Marxism to study China's social, political, economic and Chinese revolution. But he was also a "superfluous person", a so-called "traitor". In his last post "superfluous words" written in prison before his death, the personal experience revealed in it had formed a strong contrast and conflict with the current of the times, which provides a topic for future generations to ponder and continue to speak.

Under Zhang Guotao's pen, Chen Duxiu, Chen Yannian and Chen Qiaonian were three fathers and sons. They were both members of the CPC Central Committee and the main leaders of the early CPC. Chen Duxiu was reappointed as the first five general secretaries of the CPC. In the modern history of China, the history of the CPC was unique. Chen Yannian and Chen Qiaonian were once the important posts at the provincial and ministerial level of the Communist Party of China. They were killed in Longhua prison in Shanghai one after another. They all wrote seven-step poems extemporaneously before their sentence, leaving unique writing. They were so heroic that they looked at death as if they were going home. Qiaonian refused to kneel down, was cut to death by random knives, and died bravely. At that time, the white-haired people sent the black-haired people, and the father and son of the Chen family composed a unique Chinese Red historical lament, which shocked the world and wept for ghosts and gods.

In my recollections, Zhang Guotao asked Qu Qiubai about his "defection". He predicted that Qu Qiubai's question would come out one day, because both of them were representatives of the Communist Party of China stationed in the Communist International in Moscow. They lived together day by day and knew each other very well. Now, Qu Qiubai had been carrying on the suspicion of "traitor" black pot for more than half a century, and had been "pacified", and the accusation had been officially "mistaken".

In the summer of 1920, Zhang Guotao participated in the planning of Chen Duxiu and Li Dazhao, initiated and organized the Chinese branch of the Comintern, which was actually the predecessor of the Communist Party of China, and immediately launched the party building work and workers' movement. In 1921, Zhang Guotao attended the first National Congress of the Communist Party of China and was elected president of the Congress. The Congress elected him as one of the only three central committee members. The workers' movement of the Communist Party of China was founded by Zhang Guotao. Liu Shaoqi, Li Lisan, Mao Zedong, Chen Yun and others were all the same when Zhang Guotao presided over the workers' movement. At the end of 1921, Zhang Guotao, on behalf of the Communist Party of China, went to Moscow to attend the Far East people's Congress for hard work. He was the only representative of the Communist Party who met Lenin.

The historical value of My Memories was undeniable. For example, the narration of "Nanchang Uprising" and "Xi'an Incident" completely subverted people's previous understanding: after the Xi'an Incident on December 12, 1936, the CPC Central Committee discussed countermeasures, decided to instigate Zhang Xueliang and Yang Hucheng to hold a public trial bandit chieftain Chiang Kai Shek conference, Mao Zedong sent out "stinging and treacherous laughter"; when receiving the call from the Communist International strongly against the "Xi'an Incident" of Zhang and Yang, Mao Zedong was like a cold water.

The "Cultural Revolution" broke out in 1966. In October of that year, diplomats from the U.S. Consulate General in Hong Kong began to interview Zhang Guotao. When Zhang Guotao was about to leave Hong Kong, the relevant personnel from the United States visited him again, the main purpose of which was to get Zhang Guotao's analysis and judgment on the "Cultural Revolution".

The documents declassified by the U. S. government (see the air documents submitted by the U.S. Consulate General in Hong Kong to the "embassy" of the U.S. in Taipei and the Embassy in Tokyo in 1968, with the air document number of a-819, were classified into the government classified documents with the number of poll-3hk / EA / IVRS / s-053, and the original documents were stored in the Lyndon Johnson Library. The document was declassified on July 21, 1992, and then it was classified into "declassified archives of the U.S. government? Political category". It could be retrieved only by entering the "reference system of declassified archives" in major U.S. libraries or domestic libraries that had purchased the database.

Zhang Guotao made his own analysis of the reasons for the launch of the "Cultural Revolution" and its future trend that the United States was eager to know. He believed that Mao Zedong's "Cultural Revolution" had two considerations, both philosophical and power, but mainly the former. For Mao Zedong, Zhang Guotao was in a complex mood. They had known each other as early as the May 4th Movement and participated in the First National Congress of the Communist Party of China. Since then, they had been divided into two important leaders of the Soviet Union and the Red Army for a long time. In the Long March meeting decades ago, they were the protagonists of the grassland situation. For this former comrade and opponent, Zhang Guotao thought that Mao Zedong had extraordinary charm and political ability, but he was also a peasant socialist. As a peasant socialist, Mao Zedong had a desire for "equality". Once he found that the political power he built didn't provide these things, or even had the trend of going to the opposite side, with the urgency brought by the passage of time, Mao Zedong wanted to take drastic and unconventional actions to achieve the goal, that is, to prevent "change and repair", which was "cultural greatness" An important reason for the revolution.

The "Cultural Revolution" made Mao Zedong successfully clean up the opponents, but Zhang Guotao thought that although Liu Shaoqi and Deng Xiaoping had stepped down, the struggle would still exist, but only change the way. Although Mao Zedong held the highest power in the "Cultural Revolution", his main goal was not achieved. According to Zhang Guotao's analysis, Mao Zedong was an outstanding strategist rather than strategist in the "Cultural Revolution". He could not set up a transcendental theme and carry it out unremittingly. In the "Cultural Revolution", Mao Zedong was often seen to swing back and forth between policies and strategies, often trying to achieve some goals through a plan, while often affected by some emotions, and taking some dangerous dramatic actions. Zhang Guotao told the Americans that although Mao Zedong had the highest power, he doubted whether Mao Zedong could fully control everything. Lin Biao as a subordinate or others might have concealed some information from him. Zhang Guotao concluded that Mao Zedong would continue to follow the original path, but such a path would lose its effect and its original goal would not be achieved.

When it comes to Lin Biao, the heir the Americans were eager to know, Zhang Guotao thinks that he was a man of great skill, ambition, difficulty in liking and working together. One of the main reasons why Lin Biao was chosen as his successor was that Mao Zedong believed that as a subordinate who had worked for many years, Lin Biao had long-term loyalty to him. But it was clear that Lin Biao lacks the charm and political talent of Mao Zedong. Zhang Guotao speculated that if Lin Biao came to power, he would give priority to military and military interests. However, two years after the "Cultural Revolution", based on the analysis of the situation at that time, Zhang Guotao thought that Lin Biao's political advantages were somewhat specious, and his strength in the PLA seemed to be weakened, which was manifested in his inability to protect some of his close subordinates, who were defeated after the "Cultural Revolution" was launched. In Zhang Guotao's eyes, these people were Lin Biao's supporters. Although Lin Biao's authority had been weakened, Zhang Guotao believes that in the two years since the "Cultural Revolution" was launched, the role of the army had far exceeded Mao Zedong's intention to involve the army in stabilizing the situation. With the support of the army, those opponents of Mao Zedong could hardly be defeated. How to weaken the military and realize Mao Zedong's expectation would be a difficult plan. He predicted that Mao would eventually weaken the army, just as he would demobilize the red guards to the countryside. But Zhang also admitted that it would be a very difficult plan.

In addition, the Americans also asked about the trend of domestic and foreign affairs of the mainland during the "Cultural Revolution", especially about the

Revolutionary Committee, a new organization. Zhang Guotao thought that as an organization, the Revolutionary Committee had some advantages, that is, it avoided the separation between the party and the government through a single entity Revolutionary Committee, and the revolutionary committee could overcome these weaknesses to some extent. However, Zhang Guotao also doubted whether the organization could remain effective in long-term operation. Because this requires more reconstruction of the party organization in order to provide a core for the Revolutionary Committee. For the reconstruction of the party organization, Zhang Guotao believed that Mao Zedong would rely more on his former comrades in charge of party affairs, such as Chen Yun. However, Zhang Guotao thought that this kind of reconstruction seemed to be very difficult to succeed, because once it was rebuilt, Mao Zedong would worry that the state before the "Cultural Revolution" would reappear. But the "fresh blood" he sought after the "Cultural Revolution" could not provide the stability and leadership required by the party. Therefore, Zhang Guotao speculated that during the "Cultural Revolution", the party organization would still be in a mess, and it was difficult to restore its former discipline and authority.

For the diplomatic trend of mainland China during the "Cultural Revolution", Zhang Guotao thought that there was no need to think too much about the expansion of Red China. Since the "Cultural Revolution", Mao Zedong's diplomatic strategy had been continuously carried out. For example, when the Soviet Union invaded the Czech Republic, China once severely condemned it. Its purpose was to make the Soviet Union famous among socialist countries. At present, it was obvious that domestic factors were greater than foreign ones. Mao Zedong and other Chinese leaders had no time to think too much about international relations. Now foreign affairs were not a priority, even the Sino Soviet conflict and Vietnam issue were put aside. Zhang Guotao also believed that when communicating with other countries, especially western countries, Mao Zedong adopted a pragmatic approach, such as Federal Germany at that time. The reason why Mao Zedong paid attention to it was that it opposed the former Soviet Union and had the resources that China needed, and provided the goods that China badly needed. Like federal Germany, Japan, Britain and France would maintain friendly trade relations with China. Here, China would not consider the political climate at all.

How would China's political situation develop in the event of Mao Zedong's death? Zhang Guotao believed that with Mao Zedong's death, Lin Biao might inherit power, but because Lin Biao lacked the political ability, once Mao Zedong died, Lin Biao, as the successor, would cooperate well with Zhou Enlai, because Lin needed Zhou's support and expertise in governance. In Zhang Guotao's view, Zhou Enlai was a very good manager. Zhou Enlai and his deputies Li Fuchun and Li Xiannian could manage state affairs very well. Under Zhou Enlai's leadership, some doers would gradually grasp power and push the country forward. At the same time, Zhang Guotao thought that there was no "Cultural Revolution" group, including those "successors" who climbed to the top in the "Cultural Revolution" and the rebels who were capable organizers. Because of the lack of practical work ability, these "successors" would become a burden because they could not win the job.

Zhang Guotao even boldly predicted that those radicals who once surrounded Mao Zedong, such as Mao Zedong's wife, Chen Boda and Kang Sheng, would soon and effectively lose their position and political influence. In Zhang Guotao's eyes, Kang Sheng was a mediocre man who knew nothing about policy or the economy. After those radical current leaders lost their power, the more likely governance mode in China's political situation was the cooperation between Lin and Zhou. China would return to calm and enter a period of pragmatic governance. As for those who were overthrown at that time, such as Liu Shaoqi, Deng Xiaoping and so on, there would also be opportunities to return, because the governance of the country needs their experience and organizational ability.

After hearing Zhang Guotao's analysis, the officials of the U.S. Consulate General in Hong Kong left with satisfaction. A few days later, the documents about the interview were transferred to the "embassy" of the United States in Taipei and the Embassy in Tokyo, and then to the relevant departments in the United States.

In my recollections, Zhang Guotao said with deep sorrow, "on the Chinese stage, I used to be an actor, but now I am only an audience. I always hope to see fewer tragedies." This sentence was really a wake-up call, which contains a person who had experienced the rough waves of the past for the future of the nation too much and too much life perception.

Excerpt from My Memories:

I was born in a Book Family in Chengdu Plain. All I know about my family background was the image of my ancestral home Anhui, and the 13 generations of my ancestors I saw when I was a child in my hometown Qinglian Village. The first generation was during the Ming Dynasty. The people in the image wore blue robes. The next 12 generations were all officials in the Qing Dynasty. They all wore court clothes. Among them, except for one person who was a military general and who embroiders White Tigers with "Buzi" in the imperial costume, the other eleven were civil servants, who embroider white cranes on the Buzi.

When I was born, my father had already moved out of the hometown of Qinglian Lane in Chengdu, but he took us to the hometown once in a while during the new year. There were four courtyards in front of the deep mansion, and a garden in the back. There were dozens of houses. What remains in My Memories was to enter from the gate. Along the way, there were many tall Arhat pines on both sides, and the red and pleasant Arhat fruits on the trees. Then there were the large‑scale images hanging in the upper room hall, as well as many tributes placed on the tribute cases. I was afraid to kowtow. When my mother saw me hiding behind the adults, she asked me to bow three times to the image.

His father, song Zhongting, was born in Xingping County, Shaanxi Province in 1892. He went to Chengdu with his grandfather at the age of seven. Grandfather loved calligraphy and engraving seals all his life, and was very strict with his father. We should study poetry and write every day without any slack. His grandmother, Du Lanxiang, was born into a rich family and was a famous talented woman. I still had a Book of stone with all the embroidered figures paint ed by her. Grandmother was weak and had a disability in one foot. Her father was born seven months after she was pregnant. Because of her congenital deficiency, she was very weak and ill. It was said that he had a high fever when he was one year old. His grandfather was very worried. He held a medical book and couldn't sleep at night. It was like

On December 14, 1937, after the meeting of the Political Bureau of the CPC, Zhang Guotao (second from the left back) took a group photo with Mao Zedong etc

meeting an old man in a dream and telling him what medicine to take. When Grandpa woke up, he immediately sent someone to buy it and fry it for his father. It's strange to say that since then my father has recovered and grown‑up. As the saying goes, "it's hard to have only one son". Many relatives and friends advise grandfather to take a concubine. Grandfather always disagrees. Many years later, he bought Miss Sun and gave birth to an uncle.

As for my father's early life, I remember he said two things. One was a could of shrimp sauce sent by my grandfather's friend. My grandfather liked it very much. He put a spoonful of it in his father's bowl at lunch. My father didn't like shrimp sauce, but because it was given by my elder generation, I dare not not not. At last, I was forced to swallow it. The other was that my father put on a new student hat when he was in middle school and came back home happily. Grandfather saw it, frowned and said, "good hat, how to put a duck tongue, like what! Cut it off quickly. " Cut off the brim of the hat, wear out could only let students laugh, father had to put the hat in the bag, when entering the door again on the head. In his early years, his father was admitted to Tsinghua University (the predecessor of Tsinghua University). He left home alone, went north and arrived in Jiading. When he was about to board the ship, he was recovered by the people sent by his grandfather. My father wanted to go out for a long time to broaden his horizons and see the world. His failure to go north this time hit him hard. But he never gave up his desire to go out and explore the world. I often think that if he went to Tsinghua University, his life would be another scene.

My father loved English when he was a middle school student. Later, he went to a foreign language school and learned translation materials. As a result of hard work, proficient in grammar, master a large number of vocabulary, my father was known as a "walking dictionary" at that time, and taught English in several middle schools, while studying in the Foreign Language Department of Huaxi University. Later, when he graduated from Oxford University and Cambridge University, he applied to be a professor of British literature at the Chengdu Normal University, Sichuan University, West China University and other universities. At that time, there were not many people communicating with foreign letters. As long as the post office saw the mail from c.t. song from abroad, no matter whether there was an address or not, it would all send it to our home in Pifang street. I still remember when King George VI came to the throne, there were so many newspapers and magazines in those days. We always went to look at the pictures above. Queen Elizabeth was a little girl at that time.

Chapter 6 - Toronto

Toronto is located in southern Ontario, Canada, the northwestern shore of Lake Ontario. It is adjacent to New York in the southeast and Ottawa in the northeast, covering an area of 7, 125 square kilometers. Toronto is the largest city in Canada, the provincial capital of Ontario, the political, economic, cultu ral, transportation, shipping and tourism center of Canada, and a world- famous international metro polis. The city of Toronto in the heart of the Greater Toronto area and part of the

Pine Hills Cemetery's location

densely populated southern Ontario area known as the golden horseshoe area. As the economic center of Canada, Toronto is a world-class city and one of the largest financial centers in the world.

Toronto leads in finance, business services, telecommunications, aerospace, transportation, media, art, film, television production, publishing, software, pharmaceutical research, education, tourism and sports. The automobile industry, electronic industry, financial industry and tourism industry play an important role in Toronto's economy, and It's high-tech products account for 60% of Canada. The headquarters of Canada's famous big banks, such as Royal Bank, Imperial Bank, Bank of Montreal and so on, are all gathered here. Foreign bank branches in Canada, 90% are located in Toronto. Headquartered in downtown Toronto, Toronto Stock Exchange is the third largest exchange in North America and the seventh largest in the world in terms of trading volume, most Canadian companies are listed here. In addition, the famous Niagara Falls nearby attracts about 30 million tourists every year. Toronto's historic sites are now and then hidden in the modern building community, leaving clues for people to visit the past.

Golden horseshoe area is the main metropolitan area of Ontario, located in the western end of Lake Ontario. The golden horseshoe region accounts for about 25.6% of Canada's population and 75% of Ontario's population. It is one of the major metropolitan areas in North America. Its heart area extends from Niagara Falls in the east end of the Niagara Peninsula to Hamilton in the west end of Lake Ontario, and then to Oshawa in the northeast through Toronto. Generalized coverage, centered in the Greater Toronto area, extending from the lakeshore of Ontario to all sides, southwest to Brantford, West to Kitchener Waterloo area, north of Bari City, northeast of Petersburg, most of which are also above the Quebec City Windsor corridor and within the five Lake District urban agglomerations. The whole area covers an area of about 33,500 square kilometers (13,000 square miles), of which 7,300 square kilometers (2,800 square miles) are legal green areas.

When Europeans first arrived in what is now Toronto, the Huron tribe lived nearby. At that time, the tribe had replaced the Iroquois who had lived here since 1500 BC. "Toronto" may be derived from the Iroquois vocabulary tkaronto (meaning "the place where big trees grow in the middle of the water") The word comes from the fact that at the northern end of Lake SIMCO, the Huron people once planted saplings to surround the fish. From Lake Ontario to Lake Huron, a water land intermodal route now passes by here, called the Toronto line, which later became widely known.

Before 1720, Seneca Indians always lived in Toronto. Then the French set up a fur trading post in western Toronto, later France handed over it to Britain. In 1750, French merchants established a fort (Fort rouillé) at the site of the present-day Canadian exposition (CNE), which was abandoned in 1759. During the American War of independence, colonists loyal to the British Empire fled to settle in the undeveloped areas in the north of Ontario. In 1787, the British and the native Mississaugas agreed to purchase an area equivalent to the current Toronto City and York District, so they obtained more than 250,000 acres (about 1,000 square kilometers) of land in the Toronto area.

In 1793, Governor John Graves Simco established the town of York on the existed settlements, named after York and Prince Frederick, Duke of Albany. The British took Yorktown (now Toronto) as the capital of Upper Canada and renamed the emerging"York Village". Because the streets here are full of mud, Toronto also has the title of "Muddy York". In order to reduce the military threat from the United States, Simco decided to move the capital of Upper Canada from Newark, which is one river away from the United States, to York. A natural port is blocked by a long peninsula formed by sand and stone, and the authorities built Fort York at the west entrance to the harbor, the townspeople of settlements are concentrated in the eastern end of the port.

During the American British war in 1812, the U.S. Army captured York town in 1813 and plundered it. Within five days of occupying York Town, the U.S. Army burnt down the parliament building and completely destroyed York fort. This makes Britain very angry. The British fought back to Washington and set the White House on fire. The White House was named after the United States painted the building white to cover the fire. After the war, York began to expand. The new mayor changed York's name to Toronto, which means "Party Place" in the local Indian language.

York Town officially became the city of Toronto on March 6, 1834, with a population of only 9,000, including African slaves who fled from the United States. William Lyon McKenzie became the first mayor of Toronto and led the people against the British colonial government in the 1837 uprising in Canada. Toronto grew rapidly in the late 19th century. The Irish famine caused a large number of Irish to flow into Toronto from 1846 to 1849, so the Irish became the largest ethnic group in Toronto in 1851.

The capital of the United province of Canada was twice located in Toronto: the first was between 1849 and 1852, after the riots in Montreal; the second was between 1856 and 1858. After that, the government moved its capital to Quebec City. It did not move to Ottawa until 1866 (the year before the formal establishment of the Canadian Federation). Ontario was founded in 1867 and its provincial capital is Toronto. From the end of the 19 th century to the beginning of the

20th century, the immigrants to Toronto were mainly Germans, Italians and Jews from Eastern Europe. Immigrants from Chinese, Russians, poles and other Eastern European countries later arrived one after another, make the population grow rapidly.

After World War II, refugees from Eastern Europe, as well as Chinese, Italians and Portuguese arrived one after another. More immigrants arrived in Toronto from all corners of the world after the Canadian government abolished the racial discrimination immigration law in the late 1960s. Toronto's population passed the one million mark in 1951 and increased to two million in 1971. Many national enterprises and multinational enterprises in Canada, in the 1980s due to Quebec's political instability, have moved the headquarters from Montreal to Toronto, as well as other cities in Western Canada, resulting in Toronto from 1980 began to replace Montreal as the country's largest city and financial center.

From "Muddy York", the second-largest city on the Niagara River, to today's international metropolis, Toronto's growth path was not smooth. Toronto that the former name was "York", in addition to its name reminiscent of Britain's "Yorkshire", there was hope to establish a meaning than New York of United States, more prosperous cities. But for more than 200 years, "York" had not gained the slightest advantage, and even its name had been forced to give up. Because of the mud everywhere in the early days of the city's construction, got the nickname "Muddy York", "York"s people were very upset. What saddens "Yorkers" most was that their English people of the ancestral family had been unable to find out exactly where " York" were and often mistake "York" for "New York". Even some people call "York" as "Small York" (the implication is that New York of United States is "Big York"), so as to make a difference. These derogatory names forced "York" to change its name, and the relationship between "York" and "New York" ended.

Toronto is an autonomous city with a Council of mayors. The Toronto City Act gives Toronto, the largest city in Canada, greater power and freedom in the formulation of municipal bylaws and the collection of new taxes, and ensures more accountability and transparency in the operation of multi city governments. The mayor of Toronto is directly elected by the public. The Toronto City Council is a unicameral legislature composed of members from different parts of the city. The term of office of the mayor and the members of the committee is 4 years, and they can be reappointed without limit of times (originally 3 years, 2006 changed in 4 years)

Toronto has a large number of immigrants. 50% of the residents in the urban area are immigrants from more than 100 nationalities from all over the world. In 2019, the urban population of Toronto is 2.8 million (6.21 million in the Greater Toronto area) It is also a famous Chinese settlement in North America, with more than 400,000 Chinese. The arrival of new immigrants has brought a lot of money and strengthened its position as Canada's economic, commercial, financial and cultural center. The multi-ethnic characteristics make it one of the most diversified cities in the world with more than 140 languages. Toronto's international population shows that it is an important destination for new immigrants arriving in Canada. Because of its low crime rate, rich society, pleasant environment, high living standard and multi-cultural inclusiveness, Toronto has been rated as one of the most livable cities in the world by UN-Habitat for many years, occupying the top five global livable cities. At the same time, Toronto is also one of the safest, richest and most living standards cities in the world. Draw a range according to a two-hour drive from downtown Toronto, roughly one-third of Canadians live in the area. About one-sixth of Canada's jobs are in the city. The Chinese population here is the highest in the country, with immigrants from China taking the lead for many years. In addition to the two official languages of Canada, English and French, Chinese is the third largest language in Canada.

Zhang Guotao died in 1979 and his wife Yang Zilie died in 1994 in Scarborough, Ontario, Canada. Now it belongs to the Scarborough District of Toronto. Zhang Guotao and his wife were buried in Pine Hills Cemetery of Scarborough.

Before 1998, Toronto had three forms: Toronto (small-Toronto-city), metropolitan Toronto (great-Toronto-city) and Greater Toronto area (great-Toronto-area) The original city of Toronto was also called "small-Toronto-city" by local Chinese, Together with the neighboring East York, Etobicoke, North York, York and Scarborough, it was known as the great-Toronto- city, the great-Toronto - city with the neighboring Peel area, York area, the Holton area, the Dulin area

together was known as the Greater Toronto area. In 1998, in order to reduce levels, improve efficiency, save taxpayers' money and enhance the competitiveness of the city, the six cities of the Greater Toronto were merged into the "city of Toronto", a process known as the "six city merger". After the merger of six cities, Toronto had become the fifth largest city in North America, ranking second only to Mexico City, New York, Los Angeles and Chicago.

Before the merger of six cities, if we say "Toronto" without explanation, we usually mean "small-Toronto- city"; after the merger of six cities, if we say "Toronto" without explanation, we usually mean the original "great-Toronto- city".

The original "small-Toronto-city", the standard name after the merger of six cities was "Toronto District of Toronto City", also known as "old Toronto". The administrative area of "old Toronto" was very irregular, generally a large part in the South and a small part in the north. One was north to St Clair Ave, South to Lake Ontario, West to Jane st, east to Victoria ave; the other was north to Wilson Ave, South to St Clair Ave, West to Bathurst St, east to Bayview Ave. The administrative divisions of the administrative area of Toronto are relatively regular, from Steeles Ave in the north, Lake Ontario in the south, Etobicoke Creek and Road 427 in the West and Rouge River in the East. The Pine Hills Cemetery where Zhang Guotao's couple's tomb is located is in the Scarborough District of Toronto.

The downtown of Toronto refers to a block from Xiaoduo city to Bloor St in the north, Lake Ontario in the south, Bathurst St in the West and partnership St in the East before the merger of six cities; after the merger of six cities, it refers to a block from most cities to Bloor St in the north, Lake Ontario in the south, Dufferin St in the West and Don Valley Parkway Expressway (DVP) in the East.

Because the name "Toronto" has a great influence in the world, some institutions are only around the city of Toronto (usually belonging to the Greater Toronto area), and also named "Toronto". For example, the "Toronto International Airport" is located in Mississauga city in the regional municipality of peel. The Etobicoke District of Toronto only one border. Another example is the University of Toronto, which has three campuses: St George's main campus (UT / UTSG), Scarborough (UTSC) and Mississauga (UTM). St. George's main campus is located in Toronto District; Scarborough campus is located in Scarborough district; Mississauga campus is not located in Toronto City and belongs to the Greater Toronto area.

Chapter 7-Pine Hills Cemetery

Pine Hills cemetery and functional center are located in the District of Scarborough, with moderate location and convenient transportation. Founded in 1928, it is located in the Scarborough District in the southeast of Toronto. It is a rectangle, covering an area of about 0. 7 square kilometers (more than 3, 000 mu), burying tens of thousands of souls. Its auditorium and reception center covers more than 17,000 square feet. It is more than 30 kilometers away from the downtown of Toronto, one of the ten cemeteries under the Mount Pleasant Group of cemeteries, located at 625 Birchmount Rd (near St. Clair Ave. E) , and only 3 kilometers away from Lake Ontario, one of the five Dalian lakes in North America. The trees are verdant, the roads are neat, gulls are flying in the air, squirrels are playing on the ground, and they are quiet and solemn. The environment here is beautiful and quiet, and the terrain is flat and vast. In the north, it faces the 401 highway of Canada's economic artery, and in the south, it is adjacent to the rippling Lake Ontario. In addition to the burial garden for the common people, there is a special area for the cemetery of veterans, which provides more than 6, 000 veterans and spouses of Canada and allies with a symbolic fee to " home " in order to recognize and commemorate their special contributions to the country. Every September, it is a place for memorial service and memorial services for veterans. In the Second World War, the display of cannon in Qiuyuan is a

unique view of the Pine Hills Cemetery. In the tomb area, security personnel drive slowly to patrol from time to time, and workers spray water on the green grass. The urn here is buried underground, most of the tombstones and epitaphs are very striking. The cemetery has an innovative integrated visit, Chapel, reception center and product exhibition room, two condolence rooms, two reception rooms connecting the outdoor terrace, and unique audio-visual equipment for relatives and friends to watch the photos or live clips of the deceased for mourning. The chapel and reception center are spacious, providing a bright, open and comfortable atmosphere. At the same time, they are equipped with floor glass curtain walls. The sliding doors can lead to the outdoor private terrace and outdoor waterscape. The chapel is

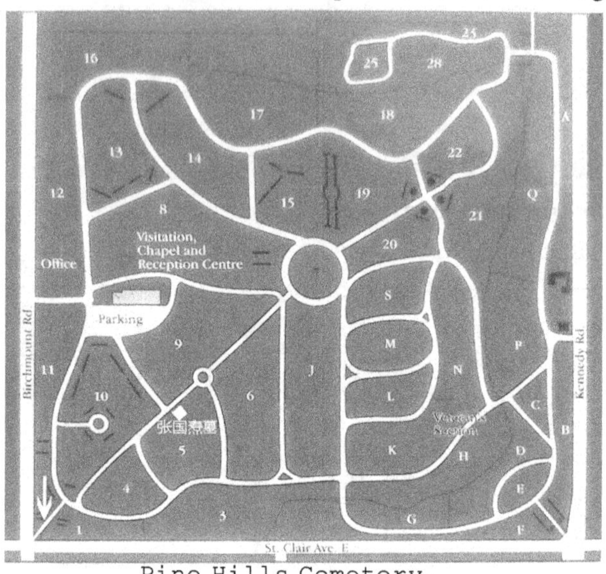

Pine Hills Cemetery,
Zhang Guotao's Tomb # 5-2263

designed by Chinese architects and integrates the concept of Geomancy. The chapel has a high ceiling and full glass walls, allowing sunlight to flow into the church, with warm wooden walls, providing a perfect atmosphere for the memorial service. The cemetery also has movable incense burners, and various kinds of sacrificial offerings are sold for the convenience of Chinese people to worship their ancestors.

The cemetery management office is a very beautiful building, with clear windows, light blue carpet, elegant flowers and green plants in the hall, creating an atmosphere of a five-star hotel. Several staff behind the counter have been busy. They will greet the guests warmly when they arrive. If the guest has a request, according to the procedure, the staff will help to start all kinds of searches in the computer system.

Since its opening, Pine Hills Cemetery has planted more than 17,000 trees and shrubs, such as maple, black cherry and elm. In the cemetery, the Massey creek winds and flows, and birds and other wild animals live in the cemetery. The numerous flower beds make the environment more peaceful. Inside, the tomb of Christ is the white marble main gate of Italy, with Christ statue inside. The cemetery provides a series of burial options such as burial, cremation, auditorium and reception center, as well as "one-stop" service and a variety of ground burial options, ranging from a single tomb to the large family cemetery. Funerals, receptions, Chapel services, visits can all be held in the same place.

Among them, the ninth district is particularly striking, with two tall monuments, one of which is the memorial to the lineage of Hongmen and the other is the memorial to the overseas Chinese in Xinhui county. At present, the Zhigong party, one of the eight major democratic parties in China, was formerly known as a Hongmen Zhigong party.

Hongmen in Canada is also a legal organization officially registered. Sun Yat-sen, the forerunner of the 1911 Revolution, there was historical enmity with Hongmen.

According to the original records of the funeral of Zhang Guotao and his wife, when Zhang Guotao was buried, Yang Zilie took care of the affairs as a relative. Her residential address at that time was 1700 Finch Avenue East, Seneca Hill Apartment for the elderly.

The joint burial cemetery of Zhang Guotao and his wife Yang Zilie was located in the fifth area of Pine Hills Cemetery (Section 5, lot 2263), next to the path in the cemetery, the tombstone is surrounded by two small pine trees. This is a joint tombstone shared by two families. The inscriptions of Zhang Guotao and his wife are on the inner side, and on the outer side of the inscriptions are the couple with the surname of Black.

The main entrance of Pine Hills Cemetery is located at 625 Birchmount Road, and the back door is located at 540 Kennedy Road. In addition, there are three side doors in the southwest corner, southeast corner and northeast corner that are not accessible for cars and only for pedestrians. Zhang Guotao's tomb is located in the northeast corner of the fifth area of Pine Hills Cemetery. If you drive a car, it is more convenient to enter the cemetery of Zhang Guotao from the front door of 625 Birchmount Road. If you are walking or cycling, you can take the Toronto Metro Line 2 (Bloor Danforth line, also known as the "Green Line Metro") to the warden metro station, change to bus No.17, follow St Clair Ave to the East and get off at the Birchmount Road Station (turning North). On the right hand side of the car is the southwest corner of Pine Hills Cemetery. It is the simplest way to get into Zhang Guotao cemetery from here Jie.

The reception hall of the Pine Hills Cemetery

The front door of Pine Hills Cemetery

The back door of Pine Hills Cemetery

The side door to the southwest
corner of Pine Hills Cemetery

Bus No.17 St
Clair / Birchmount station

Chapter 8-Tombstones of the Couple

According to the Canadian tradition, people usually hold a farewell ceremony for their dead relatives and friends at the funeral home.

The Zhang Guotao's memorial ceremony was held in a funeral home called Paul O' Connor (939 Lawrence Ave East, Scarborough). When Zhang Guotao was buried, Yang Zilie took care of the later affairs as a relative. Use Kai Yin (Kaiyin is Zhang Guotao's style name) to register in the cemetery company.

The tombstones of Zhang Guotao and his wife are ordinary gray stones, 37 $\times$ 24 $\times$ 8 inches in height, width and thickness according to the British system, 94 $\times$ 61 $\times$ 20.3 cm in the metric system, and 5 meters away from the roadside. Beside the tombstone is two small pine trees, tightly close to the stone tablet tightly, the inscription faces to the southeast.

Zhang couple's tombstone is shared with others. In the back of the monument, carved inscriptions in an old foreigner couple buried on the other side.

As a rule, the face of the tombstone seen on the side of the road is the front, and the face of the tombstone seen in the middle of the cemetery in the back. The inscriptions of Zhang Guotao and his wife are on the back.

In the original archives of Pine Hills Cemetery, the funeral records of Zhang Guotao and his wife are as follows (the Chinese in brackets is the author's note):

Name of the deceased: Kai Yin Chang

Age: (vacant)

Date of death: December 3, 1979

Date of burial: December 4, 1979

Place of birth: China

Place of death: Scarborough

Cause of death: (vacancy)

Burial permit issued by: B. Pile (shall be the relevant government staff at that time)

Priest: (the person who presides at a funeral; a vacancy)

Funeral home: Paul O'Connor

Cemetery: Pine Hills Cemetery

Nearest relative: Mrs. Tze Li Chang (wife)

1700 finch Avenue East Willowdale, Ontario (address)

Name of the deceased: Tze Li Chang

Age: 91

Date of death: March 27, 1994

Date of burial: March 9, 1994

Place of birth: China

Place of death: Toronto

Cause of death: (vacancy)

Burial permits issued: (vacant)

Priest: (the person who presides at a funeral; a vacancy)

Funeral home: (vacant)

Cemetery: Pine Hills Cemetery

Nearest relative: (vacant)

Cemetery: Pine Hills Cemetery

Nearest relative: (vacant)

It can be seen from the above data:

Zhang Guotao died on December 4, 1979, and was buried on December 5, 1979 the day after his death.

The Pinyin name Kuo Tao Chang on Zhang Guotao's tombstone (as shown in the figure: the surname Chang is engraved on the top of the tombstone, the surname in the English name originals shall be at the end), which is consistent with the author's English name record in his autobiography My Memories; the tombstone shows that he was born on November 26, 1897, and died on December 3, 1979. The English name

68

inscribed on the tombstone of Yang Zilie is Tze Li young Chang (Zhang Yang Zilie). She was born on December 9, 1902, and died on March 27, 1994.

Zhang Guotao and his wife left Hong Kong for the United States in 1966. They should hold an English passport issued by the Hong Kong government. At that time, the only official language of Hong Kong was English Kuo Tao Chang and Tze Li Young's Pinyin adopted the Weishi Spelling at that time. This is the Chinese character phonetic system "Weitouma Pinyin", which was created by Weitouma (1818-1895), a professor of Chinese at Cambridge University, to facilitate foreigners (mainly those who use English) to learn and master Chinese. This "Weitouma Pinyin" has been the English spelling method of people's names and place names used in mainland China until 1979. Later widely use Chinese Pinyin.

When Zhang Guotao was buried, he was registered in the name of Zhang Kaiyin instead of his real name, which might have been deliberately arranged by Yang Zilie, To avoid people looking for tombs.

Most of the tombstones in Pine Hills Cemetery are used alone, and the coffins are buried in front of the tombstones.

The front of the tombstone of Zhang Guotao and his wife is that of an old couple of foreigners (Tomb of George Black and his wife):
BLACK
INLOVING MEMORY OF
EVEREST | GEORGE
ABSENT FROM THE BODY
PRESENT WITH THE LORD

The inscription describes the date of birth and death of Geroge black and his wife Everest. Because the inscription does not introduce a resume, it is unknown what the background of the couple is. By comparison, the last person to die was Mrs. Black, who died in February 2000. That is to say, according to the chronological reasoning, the monument was actually updated and engraved for the last time in 2000, which should be six years later than the time when Zhang Guotao and his wife were buried together.

This is only the koizuka for storage dead clothes and hats of Zhang Guotao. His tomb is 15 meters east of here.

Chapter 9 - Stele lying on the ground

Before Yang Zilie died and was buried with Zhang, in accordance with the traditional Chinese funeral customs, as Zhang Guotao, he should at least there is also an independent original tombstone.

15 meters to the east of the tombstone, there is a very humble and easy to be ignored tombstone, which is only the size of bricks, grayish brown, all in English, with the letter Kai Yin Cheung, the person who erected the tombstone and the year when it was erected. He was a priest, not Yang Zilie, the wife of Zhang Guotao, who died 15 years later. Kaiyin, this is a popular way to spell Weishi. Kaiyin is the name of Zhang Guotao.

The monument is 40 cm away from the road and 23.7 meters away from the sign in the northeast corner of zone 5.

Because some of the steles are covered with soil, weeds and leaves, all the inscriptions can't be seen clearly.

In September 2019, the author of this book specially brought shovels, rags, buckets, etc. for cleaning. The author also brought a tape measure to measure certain distances accurately:

First remove the leaves:

Use a shovel to remove the soil and weeds that cover the monument:

Fill a bucket with water from a nearby pipe:

Clean the stele lying on the ground with a rag:

Finally, all the inscriptions on the stele are presented:

INLOVING MEMORY OF
KAI-YIN CHEUNG
One thousand nine hundred and ninety-one
FROM
FATHER: EMIL

74

MOTHER: KAREN

SISTER: ADA

2380 (the number of the tombstone in the cemetery)

In his later years, Zhang Guotao lived in a nursing home and became a Christian under the influence of volunteers. Therefore, the pastor Emil is responsible for the inscription, which is reasonable. At the same time, it objectively also had the effect of avoiding suspicion for his wife Yang Zilie.

The real Tomb of Zhang Guotao is next to the stele lying on the ground. Several feet under the earth, burying his soul, rather than the tombstone that people see now. The latter is only the second tombstone made by the descendants of Yang's family in the mid-1990s after the death of Yang Zilie. It is arranged orderly and placed nearby according to the unified management of the cemetery.

Where are the descendants of Zhang Guotao now living? Can more detailed historical data be disclosed about Zhang Guotao's later life in Toronto? Who can help solve some doubts? Many people are very interested in it. After Zhang Guotao's death, his family members disappeared. In recent years, some people have inquired about the whereabouts of their descendants from a number of overseas Chinese leaders of the Chinese community, all of which are unknown.

However, it is said that Ms. Gong Ming, a descendant of the wife of Zhang Guotao - Ms. Yang Zilie"s sister, lives in Toronto. Her grandmother, Yang Ziyu, was Yang Zilie's full sister, who immigrated to Canada in 1999. Gong Guangyan, Gong Ming's father, wrote to her that he always had a wish to contact Zhang Guotao's descendants. As relatives, it's better to meet each other. In June 2006, Gong Guangyan once lived in Toronto for a short time when he visited his relatives. The father and daughter also inquired in many ways, but there was no result

.Over the years, Gong Ming has been trying to find any clues about the descendants of Zhang Guotao. Later, she was excited by the news that Chang Guotao had a cemetery in Toronto. After all, the search for relatives had progressed. Gong Ming said that the family had the habit of regularly sweeping tombs for the deceased, and every year during the Spring Festival, the Qingming Festival and the Mid Autumn Festival.

Gong Guangyan, born in 1931 in Hubei Province, was a researcher of the soil and Fertilizer Research Institute of Henan Academy of Agricultural Sciences. He was mainly engaged in the research of soil agrochemistry and compound fertilizer. After retirement, he continued to engage in agricultural technology popularization.